Advertisement

Writing about Americans comes to be very much what is natural to any one thinking that it is pleasant to be one.

America is interesting because they will come to like a pleasant thing as they have come to be one. And every little helps.

And Useful Knowledge has been put together from every little that helps to be American. Once in talking and saying that in America the best material is used in the cheapest things because the cheapest things have to be made of the best material to make them worth while making it, it is really that it has come to be a romantic thing that has been so added to the history of living for a whole generation. It is. Romance is everything and the very best material should make the cheapest thing is making into living the romance of human being.

This is the American something that makes romance everything. And romance is Useful Knowledge.

Useful Knowledge is pleasant and therefore it is very much to be enjoyed. When there are many Americans and there are there is a great deal of pleasure in knowing that not only do they differ from one another but that Iowa and California are very pleasant and very different from one another.

And then this further, when they are altogether and ten years older and ten years younger they own the earth just as pleasantly as ever. It is nice to own the earth just as pleasantly as ever and to have Iowa and California and New York and Florida be different from one another.

Any one wishing to add a state can add one.

Singing her favorite song, "On the Trail of the Lonesome Pine," at Bilignin, summer 1937. (Photo by W. G. Rogers. Courtesy Yale Collection of American Literature, Beinecke Library.)

GERTRUDE STEIN GERTRUDE

USEFUL KNOWLEDGE USEFUL
KNOWLEDGE USEFUL KNOWL
EDGE USEFUL KNOWLEDGE
USEFUL KNOWLEDGE USEFUL
KNOWLEDGE USEFUL KNOWL
EDGE USEFUL KNOWLEDGE
USEFUL KNOWLEDGE USEFUL
KNOWLEDGE USEFUL KNOWL
EDGE USEFUL KNOWLEDGE
USEFUL KNOWLEDGE USEFUL
KNOWLEDGE USEFUL KNOWL
EDGE **USEFUL** KNOWLEDGE
USEFUL **KNOWLEDGE** USEFUL
KNOWLEDGE USEFUL KNOWL
EDGE USEFUL KNOWLEDGE
USEFUL KNOWLEDGE USEFUL
KNOWLEDGE USEFUL KNOWL
EDGE USEFUL KNOWLEDGE
USEFUL KNOWLEDGE USEFUL
KNOWLEDGE USEFUL KNOWL
EDGE USEFUL KNOWLEDGE
USEFUL KNOWLEDGE USEFUL
KNOWLEDGE USEFUL KNOWL
EDGE USEFUL KNOWLEDGE
USEFUL KNOWLEDGE USEFUL
KNOWLEDGE USEFUL KNOWL

GERTRUDE STEIN GERTRUDE STEIN

STEIN GERTRUDE STEIN GERTRUDE STEIN

GERTRUDE STEIN GERTRUDE

FOREWORD BY EDWARD BURNS
INTRODUCTION BY KEITH WALDROP

STATION HILL PRESS

Published by Station Hill Press, Inc., Barrytown, New York 12507, with grateful acknowledgement to the National Endowment for the Arts, a federal agency in Washington, D.C., and the New York State Council of the Arts, for partial financial support of this project.

Acknowledgement: The publisher wishes to thank Mr. Dick Higgins for calling attention to this book and supplying the original edition.

Produced by the Institute for Publishing Arts, Barrytown, New York 12507, a not-for-profit, tax-exempt organization.

Designed by Susan Quasha and George Quasha.

Distributed by the Talman Co., Inc., 150 Fifth Avenue, New York, New York 10011.

Library of Congress Cataloging-in-Publication Data

Stein, Gertrude, 1874-1946.
    Useful knowledge / Gertrude Stein ; foreword by Edward Burns ; introduction by Keith Waldrop.
        p. cm.
        ISBN 0-88268-075-7
        I. Title.
    PS3537.T323U7   1988   88-24766
    811'.52—dc19   CIP

Manufactured in the United States of America.

CONTENTS

Foreword

Useful Knowledge about Useful Knowledge

The pieces collected in *Useful Knowledge* were not written with the intention of forming a specific, unified book. This was Gertrude Stein's first volume to be published in America since *Geography and Plays* in 1922. She wanted to reach out to an American audience, and perhaps in an effort to do so, she selected works that reflected the theme of America. The pieces she chose speak to her pride in being an American. "Writing about Americans," she says, "comes to be very much what is natural to any one thinking that it is pleasant to be one."

From the time she settled in France in 1903 until her death there in 1946, Stein's writings return, again and again, to the people and landscape of her native land. At the beginning of her career stand the immigrant servants and blacks in *Three Lives*, as well as the history of her own family's leaving the old world for the new which she recounts in *The Making of Americans*. At the end of her life comes the broad canvas of historical figures, contemporaries, and imagined characters of *The Mother of Us All*—her opera about Susan B. Anthony.

Gertrude Stein did not consider herself an expatriate living in exile. On the modest income that her eldest brother Michael managed for her, she enjoyed a life that would have been difficult to match in the United States. Stein, in Paris, was never far from her native land as Joyce was never far from his.

Into *Useful Knowledge* she placed compositions about American landscape and places; she also included portraits of contemporary figures such as Woodrow Wilson, Paul and Eslanda Robeson, Josephine Baker and members of the music-hall show *La Revue Nègre*; and portraits of her friends Carl Van

Vechten, Emily Chadbourne, Allen Tanner, and Emmet Addis. Some of Stein's experiences during the First World War, when she drove a supply truck for the American Fund for French Wounded are to be found here. There are also evocations of childhood as in "Lend a Hand or Four Religions." And always, her life with Alice Toklas becomes the emblem of ecstasy.

Whether Stein took the title *Useful Knowledge* from the series of French school *cahiers* entitled *La Parole du Maître (Connaissances Utiles)* or whether it was associated in her mind with remembered American experience or reading is not clear. Stein often played with titles and phrases from the *cahiers* in her writing.

The majority of the pieces in *Useful Knowledge* had not been published. Only the poems "A Patriotic Leading," "A League," and "More League" (originally titled "Two Cubist Poems. The Peace Conference I"), and the longer compositions "Van or Twenty Years After; a Second Portrait of Carl Van Vechten," and "Idem the Same: A Valentine to Sherwood Anderson," had previously been published.

The Van Vechten portrait and the "Valentine" to Anderson pay tribute to two of Stein's close friends and early supporters. Van Vechten first met Stein when he brought her a letter of introduction from Mabel Dodge, who maintained an important New York salon in the years just before World War I. Van Vechten, a young journalist and critic, met Stein in May 1913. From that day until his death in 1964, his loyalty and devotion to Stein and then Toklas were immeasurable. The portrait of Van Vechten printed here was completed in Nice in September 1923. Stein's idea was to complement the first portrait she had written in 1913 of him.

"Idem the Same: A Valentine to Sherwood Anderson" was first printed in *The Little Review* in the Spring of 1923. The issue was assembled by Margaret Anderson and Jane Heap with work of writers and artists who were at "[P]resent pleasantly exiled in Europe." Among them were Ernest Hemingway, Mina Loy, George Antheil, E.E. Cummings, Jane Heap, H.D., Robert McAlmon, Dorothy Shakespear, and Joan Miró. The term exile was taken to mean foreigners living in France. Non-exiles Jean Cocteau and Fernand Léger were also represented.

The "Valentine" gives us an insight into Stein's methods of composition. The piece had a special meaning for her. It was one of the pieces that she recorded at Columbia University in 1935; the recording is still available.

Sherwood Anderson's reputation was growing when he first met Stein in the Fall of 1921. His first acquaintance with her writing was probably her portraits, "Pablo Picasso" and "Henri Matisse," published in the August 1912 issue of Alfred Stieglitz's *Camera Work*. He soon read Stein's *Three Lives* and then, thanks to his brother, he read her *Tender Buttons*. All of this was before he met her.

Anderson and his wife Tennessee sailed for France on 14 May 1921. From Sylvia Beach, the proprietor of the bookshop Shakespeare and Company, Anderson received a letter of introduction to Stein. At the time that Stein and Anderson met, Stein had just arranged for a Boston publisher, Four Seas Company, to bring out a collection of her work. Although Anderson was known in literary circles, he was not yet a "celebrity" whose presentation of a work would add to its merit in the eyes of the public. Stein was moved by Anderson's admiration for her work; at her request, he agreed to write a foreword for her book *Geography and Plays*. In "The Work of Gertrude Stein," he affectionately recounted his discovery of her work and what it meant to him. From New Orleans, in February 1922, Anderson sent Stein his text. It was accompanied by a brief message, "I could write a volume and not in the end say more. I hope you'll like it."

From the manuscript of the "Valentine," in a French school *cahier*, it appears that the piece may have been begun before the arrival of Anderson's foreword, which became the impetus for a new title. The top of the first page of the *cahier* reads:

A/V̶a̶l̶e̶n̶t̶i̶n̶e̶
Idem the same
A Valentine To
A̶/̶P̶o̶r̶t̶r̶a̶i̶t̶/̶o̶f̶ Sherwood Anderson

"Idem the same" may refer to Stein's change from the idea of "portrait of" to "Valentine To," echoing what may have been the original title, "A Valentine." There is a suggestion of school-room recitation and memorizing in the Latin term *Idem* followed by its meaning—the same. Stein's final title makes it clear that this is not a portrait of Anderson, but rather something being offered to him as a valentine, perhaps as a thank-you for his foreword.

Like so many of Stein's compositions, this piece is about many things. It is, I think, in celebration of Stein's domestic life with Alice Toklas—perhaps the intended recipient of the original valentine. In the manuscript section of "A VERY VALENTINE," the word "mine" was, in all but one instance, originally written as "Stein." This is only one of several examples in the manuscript that suggest Stein intended the piece as a meditation on herself and Alice Toklas.

The manuscript also makes clear that Stein perceived a specific shape for the piece. When she finished the composition, she went through it making several changes and deletions. At the end of certain sections, she inserted "(Space)" to guide Toklas as she typed.

Given the dual personal impulses behind this piece and its title, it is all the more interesting to contemplate how it came to be truncated. As printed, the piece lacks its two concluding sections—which are included in other printings. There is nothing in the correspondence nor does Joseph Brewer remember any exchange about these lines. It is possible that a

x

careless typesetting error was not picked up by Stein and Toklas when they read proofs. Here, then, are the concluding sections of the piece.

IN THIS WAY

Keys please, it is useless to alarm any one it is useless to alarm some one it is useless to be alarming and to get fertility in gardens in salads in heliotrope and in dishes. Dishes and wishes are mentioned and dishes and wishes are not capable of darkness. We like sheep. And so does he.

LET US DESCRIBE

Let us describe how they went. It was a very windy night and the road although in excellent condition and extremely well graded has many turnings and although the curves are not sharp the rise is considerable. It was a very windy night and some of the larger vehicles found it more prudent not to venture. In consequence some of those who had planned to go were unable to do so. Many others did go and there was a sacrifice, of what shall we, a sheep, a hen, a cock, a village, a ruin, and all that and then that having been blessed let us bless it.

*   *   *

Stein's writings convey the density of her perceptions and her emotions. They also trace the writing process itself. Her work is, in part, about the method by which she utilizes and transforms the fabric of experience and memory, the bits and pieces of her "daily everyday living," into poetic constructions. For the reader, the energy and the pleasure of Stein's writing does not depend on a knowledge of these experiences. Nor does the eloquence of her poetic language depend on conventional definitions of genre.

Reading Stein is still difficult, even for a generation that has mastered Joyce, Eliot, and Pound. The traditional habits of reading, of forming emphasis, do not always help with a Stein text. Often, the textures of meaning rise from the page when these habits are avoided. Listen to Stein reading from her own works. The voice lacks almost all sense of emphasis, and yet she brings out the inner structure and sense of each piece. Her language instills an awareness of *language*—how it gives shape and meaning to what we see in daily life.

Stein's writing is dazzling in its virtuosity. It tends to be intimate—"Farragut or A Husband's Recompense"; innovative in its form—"Are There Six"; and playful—"Any one wishing to add a state can add one." Her writing can also be realistic when she recalls the First World War. In her "Advertisement" to *Useful Knowledge* she encourages the reader with the prospect that "Useful Knowledge is pleasant and therefore it is very much to be enjoyed."

*   *   *

In either the Summer or early Fall of 1926, Joseph Brewer, an enterprising young member of the American publishing firm of Payson & Clarke, approached Gertrude Stein for a manuscript. Brewer, from Grand Rapids, Michigan, had graduated from Dartmouth College in 1920, and read English Literature at Oxford University. From 1922 to 1924 he regularly contributed to the *London Spectator*. When he returned to America, he first went to work for the publishing firm of D. Appleton. But by early 1926, he had joined the firm of Payson & Clarke.

Gertrude Stein was already known to a small, discriminating audience when she made Brewer's acquaintance. By 1926, twelve books or pamphlets by Stein had been published.

Among these were: *Three Lives* (1909); *Tender Buttons* (1914); *Geography and Plays* (with the introduction by Sherwood Anderson, 1922); and *The Making of Americans* (1925). Three publications would appear in 1926: *Descriptions of Literature* (published by George Platt Lynes and Adlai Harbeck as one of their As Stable Pamphlets); *Composition as Explanation* (published by Leonard and Virginia Woolf at The Hogarth Press); and *A Book Concluding with As A Wife Has a Cow a Love Story* (published by Daniel-Henry Kahnweiler and illustrated by Juan Gris). With the help of Henry McBride, Carl Van Vechten, and Mabel Dodge, pieces by Stein had also been placed in the ever surfacing and disappearing world of small magazines and reviews.

Stein was always on the lookout for a commercial publisher. She had helped to subsidize many of her own publications either directly or indirectly by enlisting her friends and ac-quaintances as subscribers. In America, Carl Van Vechten, Stein's de-facto literary agent, tried valiantly but was unable to convince his own publisher and close friend, Alfred A. Knopf, to become Stein's American publisher. Stein believed that if her books could reach a wide audience, they would not be regarded as "hermetic." She hoped that in Joseph Brewer and the firm of Payson & Clarke she had found such a publisher.

The typescript that Stein sent Brewer in the Fall of 1926 contained texts that had been composed between 1915 and 1926. Two additional pieces, "Advertisement" and "Introducing" were added to the book in 1927. Brewer acknowledged receipt of the manuscript (a word used interchangeably for type-script) on 30 November 1926. It would take Brewer and his sympathetic partner, Edward Warren, almost two years before they would bring out the book. At the heart of their problem was how to promote an author so different in style from anything that they had previously published. Brewer commu-nicated his company's initial thinking in a letter to Stein on 7 March 1927. He proposed creating a library of books in a special format, and producing them in a limited edition. Although we do not have Stein's reply to Brewer, it is evident from his subsequent letters that Stein raised objections to a limited edition.

In September, Brewer went from London to Paris to see Stein. He asked Stein to write a "blurb" for the book (Stein's "Advertisement" which was printed on the inside flap of the dust-wrapper and in the text). It may have been during this visit that Stein gave Brewer the typescript for "Introducing."

When Brewer wrote to Stein on 17 February 1928 to thank her, he reported on the progress of publication. Payson & Clarke decided to call the series *2 Rivers*, and E. McKnight Kauffer was engaged to design the logo—a symbol of the two rivers of Manhattan. Brewer himself designed the title page.

The proofs were sent to Stein on 12 April and by 26 April Stein could write to Carl Van Vechten, who was correcting proofs for his novel *Spider Boy*, "I will like seeing your book, I too am correcting proofs, Payson & Clarke are bringing out a book of collected things, Useful Knowledge or Americana, all my or at least some of my American things collected, your portrait among them, there is one on Woodrow [Wilson] and A Hundred prominent men that I think you will like."

Stein's letter to Brewer acknowledging the proofs cannot be located, but from his response, and from drafts of Stein's later letters to Brewer, it is clear that she was pleased with the page-proofs and the design of the book. She used the opportunity of an impending publication to urge Payson & Clarke to publish more of her work. Brewer responded on 21 April that he was looking forward to reading Stein's two new works, "Finally George, a Vocabulary of Thinking," and "Arthur A Grammar" when he saw her again.

By mid-August, Stein's author's copies had gone off to her. From London, in September, Brewer wrote Stein that before he had left New York, 150 copies of the book had been sold. Payson & Clarke had printed 500 copies on a special paper; 1000 or 1500 were on an ordinary paper. This difference in paper quality allowed the publisher the option of charging a slightly higher price, $5, for the initial printing, thus in a small way satisfying their desire for a "limited edition."

Brewer did not visit Stein in Belley as she had proposed. In his letter from London, however, he wrote that he did think it possible to reprint the Hogarth Press' edition of Stein's, *Composition as Explanation*. He felt sure that the publication of this volume would help the sales of *Useful Knowledge*. Although the book's sales were not what he had expected— only 213 copies had been sold by mid-October—Brewer maintained his enthusiasm for Stein. From New York, he wrote her on 26 October that he was seriously considering *Composition as Explanation*, and that he had spoken with William A. Bradley, Stein's literary agent, about her new novel, *Lucy Church Amiably*.

Stein's long experience with reluctant publishers did not leave her open to great expectations. She had already begun circulating typescripts of *Lucy Church Amiably*. In March, she sent the novel to the English firm of Kegan Paul, Trench, Trubner & Co., Ltd., hoping it would fit into their To-day and To-morrow series.

When they returned the manuscript they wrote her, "We have read 'Lucy Church Amiably' with much interest, and given it to an expert reader; both he and we think the book is very clever, but regret to say that we do not think it has any considerable chance of selling remuneratively." This was the kind of response that Stein normally received from publishers. Still, she seized upon the phrase "with much interest" and wrote them again. From the draft of her letter, we learn that Stein offered them a smaller book that might fit into their series. She suggested they print her "Patriarchal Poetry" and "Phenomena of Nature." When he replied to this letter, Kegan Paul's representative sounded the other note that Stein had grown familiar with—he acknowledged the public interest in her "experiments," but felt it was not anything significant enough to warrant a book in their series.

Although Payson & Clarke had signed a formal agreement of affiliation with the English publisher Victor Gollancz in late 1927, it was to John Lane, publisher of The Bodley Head editions, that they sold 500 sheets of *Useful Knowledge* in the Fall of 1928. John Lane kept the title page and substituted his own firm's name at the bottom in place of Payson & Clarke's. He also dropped the publisher's page with the logo and explanation of the *2 Rivers* series. Brewer wrote to inform Stein of this sale on 15 November; in the same letter, he expressed his continued interest in *Lucy Church Amiably*.

Brewer acknowledged receipt of the manuscript in a letter to Stein of 14 December. On 18 December he again wrote to Stein, this time thanking her for the "blurb" that she had sent him for *Lucy Church Amiably*. Stein no doubt read Brewer's interest as a sure sign that he would publish the novel. She would wait several months for Brewer's reply. He wrote her on 26 March 1929, "It is ages since I wrote you . . . . We have been wrestling with desire and temptation like Saint Anthony. We should *like* someday collecting you all together & c. But the difficulty is our present position as publishers." Payson & Clarke, by now Brewer and Warren, had lost $1000 on *Useful Knowledge*; it was becoming difficult for the firm to manage as they had planned. Graciously and reluctantly, Brewer had to acknowledge that he was unable to undertake another Stein volume.

Stein's reply to Brewer has not survived. But on the back of his letter to her of 26 March are two drafts of an answer. She tried gently to coax him. She began one draft, "Yes, I think you should do Lucy Church Amiably, you do owe it to me." She felt that she had given Payson & Clarke the impetus to start the *2 Rivers* series and that, as she wrote in her second draft, "I think you should be just and I think you should do Lucy Church Amiably."

Neither Brewer nor any English or American publisher that Stein wrote to would do the novel. Even William A. Bradley, Stein's literary agent, had no luck in placing her manuscripts. By the Fall of 1929 the American stock market crash had forced retrenchment in the publishing houses. The small edition book, the book with a limited sales potential, seemed destined to give way to a new set of economic realities. Publishers needed surefire sellers if they were to survive in troubled times. Stein felt no resentment toward Brewer personally. Indeed, they renewed their friendship in 1935 when Brewer, then President of Olivet College in Michigan, invited Stein to meet his students. She recounted her visit in *Everybody's Autobiography*.

The cumulative effect of rejections and disappointments led Stein and Toklas to take a step that they had probably already contemplated. They decided to publish Stein's work themselves. They named their press the Plain Edition. Alice Toklas was to be the editor and salesperson, Stein the firm's sole author. Between 1930 and 1933 they published five volumes of Stein's work. The expense of publishing forced Stein to sell at least one painting by Picasso, and to print limited editions. The Plain Edition volumes became, over the years, sought-after collector items. Unfortunately for the reader of Stein, they also became treasures that could be read only in the Rare Book rooms of major libraries.

It was not until 1966, when Dick Higgins, founder of The Something Else Press began reprinting out of print volumes, that crucial works by Stein became available. This tradition is now being carried on by Station Hill Press, first with Stein's *Operas and Plays* (a Plain Edition book), and now with *Useful Knowledge*.

Edward Burns

Notes

The Stein-Anderson correspondence is collected in *Sherwood Anderson/Gertrude Stein: Correspondence and Personal Essays*, edited by Ray Lewis White, The University of North Carolina Press, 1972. The Joseph Brewer-Gertrude Stein correspondence is in the Collection of American Literature, Beinecke Rare Book and Manuscript Library, Yale University. I am grateful to Mr. Brewer for an interview he granted me. Kegan Paul's letters to Stein are in the Yale Collection of American Literature. The Stein-Van Vechten correspondence is collected in *The Letters of Gertrude Stein and Carl Van Vechten, 1913-1946*, edited by Edward Burns, Columbia University Press, 1986.

Introduction

Gertrude Stein's Tears

". . . the old is too old and the new is too old."
Useful Knowledge

Gertrude Stein's most striking accomplishment, moving us still to admiration or derision, is the style of the works just following *The Making of Americans*, roughly between 1907 and 1914—the style known, because of its first occasions, as the "portrait style." It would be an exaggeration, rather than an untruth, to say that she herself was so impressed by this stylistic breakthrough that she spent the rest of her life, on the one hand trying to explain to herself and others just what she had done, and—on the other—adapting the portrait style to new, on the whole more conventional, uses (the later novels, the children's books, etc.). The texts she collected as *Useful Knowledge* are from just after this breakthrough and may be best seen as celebrations of its success. Hence their tone of assurance.

Much energy has gone into deciphering words and phrases in Stein's more opaque pieces and we are told, for instance, that the words "melon," "jew," "cow," and "Caesars" are all erotic references, mostly to Alice B. Toklas.[1] I have no argument with such a claim—it seems likely enough—but would in the present essay approach the problem from a different angle, in an attempt to understand the sense of the style rather than the meanings of individual passages. After all, using the word in its ordinary sense, much of Stein's most characteristic writing "means" little or nothing.

The crucial developments in Gertrude Stein's style took

place in less than a decade, between 1906 and 1914-that is to say, while she was in her thirties. If the important stages are given schematically, they show a logical progression.

Stage 1: Struck by "the rhythm of each human being,"[2] she attempts to combine the description of character with the presentation of the character's rhythm. In "Melanctha," the last of the *Three Lives* to be written, the two main characters have life-rhythms that differ just enough to keep them always out-of-phase one to the other and to prevent their coming finally together. The speech of Melanctha and that of the Doctor are slight but significant variations on the narrative voice itself, a somewhat stylized black speech-pattern which envelops the entire story.

> If she ever needed anybody to be good to her, Jeff Campbell always would do anything he could to help her. He never can forget the things she taught him so he could be really understanding, but he never any more wants to see her. He be like a brother to her always, when she needs it, and he always will be a good friend to her. Jeff Campbell certainly was sorry never any more to see her, but it was good that they now knew each other really. "Good-by Jeff you always been very good always to me." "Good-by Melanctha you know you always can trust yourself to me." "Yes, I know, I know Jeff, really." "I certainly got to go now Melanctha, from you. I go this time, Melanctha really," and Jeff Campbell went away and this time he never looked back to her. This time Jeff Campbell just broke away and left her.[3]

Stage 2: She describes, in the *Making of Americans*, less the action of her characters, than their mode of being. Whereas in *Three Lives* she deals with characters who generate their individual and collective rhythms, she now analyzes the human rhythm into characteristic elements and the various combinations of elements make up her characters. These elements, almost always expressed in present participles, are grouped in categories—each man, for example, has his mode of "loving":

> Some men have it in them in their loving to be attacking, some have it in them to let things sink into them, some let themselves wallow in their feeling and get strength in them from the wallowing they have in loving, some in loving are melting—strength passes out from them, some in their loving are worn out with the nervous desire in them, some have it as a dissipation in them, some have it as excitement in them, some have it as a clean attacking, some have it in them as a daily living—some as they have eating in them, some as they have drinking, some as they have sleeping in them, some have it in them as believing, some have it as a simple beginning feeling—some have it as the ending always of them such of them are always old men in their loving.[4]

If then a table could be made in this way for all the elements of all the categories, one would have a complete catalog of human types or, as Gertrude Stein calls them, "natures"—with, however, the complication that a person will ordinarily have several "natures" superimposed, one of which is that person's fundamental or, in her interesting term, "bottom nature."

She does not, in *The Making of Americans*, attempt the complete catalog (though convinced of its possibility) but combines sketches towards it with the story of two families coming from Europe but made into Americans by being put into the American geography. So to the catalog of human types is added a sort of geographical explanation of those types: the rhythm of a landscape determines the rhythms of its inhabitants—a theme she will come back to again and again. (The idea will provide much of the thematic material

xxi

of *Useful Knowledge*, though the treatment there will be less expository, more musical.)

Stage 3: The Making of Americans is more abstract than *Three Lives*, in the sense that it is essayistic and discursive, generalizing its characters rather than making them concrete and particular. Except for the last chapter (which was added only in 1911) it is still representational. The language, though extremely stylized, is still transparent enough for us to see that there are in fact characters and that those characters are in some sort of situation. Before finishing *The Making of Americans*, however, she has begun her "portraits" and rapidly reaches the point where they exclude description. One can see even how it diminishes—from little to less—by moving from her portrait of Matisse (1909):

> One was quite certain that for a long part of his being one being living he had been trying to be certain that he was wrong in doing what he was doing and then when he could not come to be certain that he had been wrong in doing what he had been doing, when he had completely convinced himself that he would not come to be certain that he had been wrong in doing what he had been doing he was really certain then that he was a great one and he certainly was a great one. Certainly every one could be certain of this thing that this one is a great one.[5]

to this portrait of a dancer (1913):

> Please be please be get, please get wet, wet naturally, naturally in weather. Could it be fire more firier. Could it be so in ate struck. Could it be gold up, gold up stringing, in it while while which is hanging, hanging in dingling, dingling in pinning, not so. Not so dots large dressed dots, big sizes, less laced, less laced diamonds, diamonds white, diamonds bright, dia-

monds in the in the light, diamonds light diamonds door diamonds hanging to be four, two four, all before, this bean, lessly, all most, a best, willow, vest, a green guest, guest go go go go go go, go. Go go. Not guessed. Go go.

Toasted susie is my ice-cream.[6]

If the essential of "each human being" is a rhythm, then to express that rhythm expresses the person. There is no need actually to talk *about* the subject in any sense at all, either to present him, visually or otherwise, or to categorize him abstractly. It is as if, to be sure of getting the essence, she is willing to dispose of all the accidents—every quality can go.

The next stage is similar, but cuts off one possibility of misunderstanding.

Stage 4: She moves from "portraits" to the "still lifes" of *Tender Buttons*, turning for subjects to things rather than persons. In "Melanctha," the rhythms of the characters were expressed, naturally enough, by the characters speaking. It is conceivable— in some cases likely—that certain of the portraits attempt to imitate the subject's speech-pattern, even while saying nothing that the subject would be liable to say, or indeed saying nothing at all. When her subjects become inanimate objects, this can hardly be the case.

Here is the beginning of a section of *Tender Buttons* with the heading "Roastbeef":

In the inside there is sleeping, in the outside there is reddening, in the morning there is meaning, in the evening there is feeling. In the evening there is feeling. In feeling anything is resting, in feeling anything is mounting, in feeling there is resignation, in feeling there is recognition, in feeling there is recurrence and entirely mistaken there is pinching. All the standards have steamers and all the curtains have bed linen and all the yellow has discrimination and all the circle has circling. This makes sand.[7]

xxiii

Stage 5: A similar progress, this time from objects to events, brings her to the writing of "plays." "And the idea in *What Happened, A Play* was to express this without telling what happened, in short to make a play the essence of what happened."[8]

The problem proper to these last three stages is obvious and has often been stated—"How do you know," Edwin Arlington Robinson asked Mabel Dodge, when she showed him Stein's portrait of her, "that it is a portrait of you, after all?"[9] Gertrude Stein's own statement is later, but there seems no reason not to take it seriously:

> I became more and more excited about how words which were the words that made whatever I looked at look like itself were not the words that had in them any quality of description. This excited me very much at that time.
>
> And the thing that excited me so very much at that time and still does is that the word or words that make what I looked at be itself were always words that to me very exactly related themselves to that thing the thing at which I was looking, but as often as not had as I say nothing whatever to do with what any words would do that described that thing.[10]

Leaving aside, only for the moment, questions of purpose, we may identify the source of the peculiarities of Stein's vocabulary and syntax in her portraits, still-lifes and plays by looking at what Vygotsky says of "inner speech" in his *Thought and Language*. By the term "inner speech" he means

> speech for oneself; external speech is for others . . . . (Inner speech) is neither an antecedent of external speech nor its reproduction in memory but is, in a sense, the opposite of external speech. The latter is the turning of thought into words, its materialization

and objectification. With inner speech, the process is reversed: Speech turns into inward thought. Consequently, their structures must differ.[11]

Vygotsky found a way to study inner speech by showing that it has an earlier, still vocal, form: what Piaget had called "egocentric speech," the kind of speech where a child

> talks only about himself, takes no interest in his interlocutor, does not try to communicate, expects no answers, and often does not even care whether anyone listens to him. It is similar to a monologue in a play: The child is thinking aloud, keeping up a running accompaniment, as it were, to whatever he may be doing.[12]

By analyzing egocentric speech while it is still spoken aloud, before it "'goes underground,' i.e., turns into inner speech," Vygotsky could establish certain characteristics of inner speech.

The syntax of inner speech is simplified by the elimination of the grammatical subject. (We already "know what we are thinking about.") What is left approaches "pure predication."

> As egocentric speech develops it shows a tendency toward an altogether specific form of abbreviation: namely, omitting the subject of a sentence and all words connected with it, while preserving the predicate. This tendency toward predication appears in all our experiments with such regularity that we must assume it to be the basic syntactic form of inner speech.[13]

So Gertrude Stein, in her lecture on "Poetry and Grammar":

> As I say a noun is a name of a thing and therefore slowly if you feel what is inside that thing you do not call it by the name by which it is known. Everybody

knows that by the way they do when they are in love and a writer should always have that intensity of emotion about whatever is the object about which he writes. And therefore and I say it again more and more one does not use nouns.[14]

Emphasis on the predicate brings about a reduced vocabulary, many things being "understood," and indeed a kind of speech which Vygotsky describes as being "almost without words." That is to say, not that the flow of words is shortened—on the contrary, it tends to be of indefinite length—but merely that fewer and fewer words carry more and more sense. Note how well the portrait of Harry Phelan Gibb (1913) shows all this:

> Some one in knowing everything is knowing that some one is something. Some one is something and is succeeding is succeeding in hoping that thing. He is suffering.
> He is succeeding in hoping and he is succeeding in saying that that is something. He is suffering, he is suffering and succeeding in hoping that in succeeding in saying that he is succeeding in hoping is something.
> He is suffering, he is hoping, he is succeeding in saying that anything is something. He is suffering, he is hoping, he is succeeding in saying that something is something. He is hoping that he is succeeding in hoping that something is something. He is hoping that he is succeeding in saying that he is succeeding in hoping that something is something. He is hoping that he is succeeding in saying that something is something.[15]

Finally, there are semantic peculiarities of inner speech:

> The first and basic one is the preponderance of the *sense* of a word over its *meaning* . . . . The sense of

a word . . . is the sum of all the psychological events aroused in our consciousness by the word. It is a dynamic, fluid, complex whole, which has several zones of unequal stability. Meaning is only one of the zones of sense, the most stable and precise zone. A word acquires its sense from the context in which it appears; in different contexts, it changes its sense. Meaning remains stable throughout the changes of sense . . . .

In inner speech, the predominance of sense over meaning, of sentence over word, and of context over sentence is the rule.[16]

These descriptions of inner speech fit the portrait style of Gertrude Stein so perfectly that one is led to wonder about the single great difference: inner speech is inner, silent, private; Stein's words are outside her, on the page, in the world. I am not suggesting that she was merely talking to herself. But there would seem to be no very good reason why the style of inner speech, its formal peculiarities, cannot be adapted to writing—and as that appears to be what she has done, we may ask what purposes, aesthetic or other, such a style fulfills.

The syntax of inner speech is originally adopted by the child, says Vygotsky, because he "talks about the things he sees or hears or does at a given moment,"[17] which is immediately reminiscent of Stein's concept of a "continuous present." She professes to have been bothered always by the fact that in any narrative there is both a time in which the story takes place and another time which it takes to read or watch the unfolding story. This she labels "confusion," as the two times interfere with each other. Her own plays, for instance, are meant to have only their own time and no other—a condition she likens to the contemplation of a landscape.

I felt that if a play was exactly like a landscape then there would be no difficulty about the emotion of the person looking on at the play being behind or ahead of the play because the landscape does not have to make acquaintance.[18]

But confusion of times in literary works is only the symptom of a larger problem. Her villain is "memory," which binds us to past interpretations, making us repeat endlessly actions and perceptions that are dead and prevent us from finding our potentialities in the present.

> [I]ntelligent people although they talk is if they knew something are really confusing, because they are so to speak keeping two times going at once, the repetition time of remembering and the actual time of talking . . . .[19]

The solution is not, of course, to try to forget everything, but simply to act as a living being, taking one's cues from the entire present (which includes the remembered past) rather than acting from a set of learned or inherited instructions. As she acknowledges, this is derived from William James's teaching on "habit." In a really vital situation, "No matter how often what happened had happened any time any one told anything there was no repetition. This is what William James calls the Will to Live."[20]

This "continuous present" is not a peculiarity in the thought of the period. It is related to Gide's "*disponibilité*," Heidegger's "resoluteness," and Krishnamurti's striking motto "freedom from the known." In all these, as in Stein, the point is not not to know, but not to be held captive by what one knows—or thinks one knows.

But her solution to the literary side of the problem is her own. Ordinary life (what she calls "human nature") is an endless, hopeless repetition, at once product and producer of politics, religion, propaganda, and war—and it is controlled by age, sickness, and death. On the other hand, there is a part of us which can transcend "human nature" into a realm which is just as real, just as objective, but is a realm of pure play—she

xxviii

calls it "the human mind." Language is in between—it can be used, and also can be used for play.

The formulation is later, but the thought is consistent. The American has been shaped by a land so large as to be abstract, the very divisions being arbitrary. He has unmatched mobility, detaching him from any territory he might feel part of. The American has, furthermore, inherited a foreign language, which sits uneasily on American things. The great American writer, Henry James, had already reached the point—in his later novels—where the style and the subject almost (but not quite) separated.[21]

To complete the separation is a small step from there. Perceptions, being rhythmic, produce rhythmic responses in inner speech, but the response, removed from any further association with the things perceived, may be developed through all the laws of play. The end product, like all products of "the human mind," will be formal and abstract, though it may contain representations. And it will be the record of an exploration: This mental traveler will, as she puts it in *Useful Knowledge*, "later be able to make maps of the region which he has traversed." "I found myself," she says elsewhere,

> plunged into a vortex of words, burning words, cleans-
> ing words, liberating words, feeling words, and the
> words were all ours and it was enough that we held
> them in our hands to play with them; whatever you
> can play with is yours.[22]

And at the end of her first lecture on *Narration*:

> I like the feeling of words doing as they want to do
> and as they have to do when they live where they
> have to live that is where they have come to live which
> of course they do do.[23]

It seems to me that she made no extravagant claims. Of the worth of what she was doing, she appears to have had few doubts. She was convinced that "the human mind" made "human nature" worth living, but beyond the free play of mind, she generally conceded that things are what they are. Her style is such as to leave them where they are. In her fullest theoretical statement, *The Geographical History of America or the Relation of Human Nature to the Human Mind*, she says:

> Anybody with a human mind can say I mean and they can say I forgot and mean that. Fighting is not an action of the human mind neither is remembering if it had to do with the human mind then the human mind would concern itself with age but it does not, therefore any nature can mean or not mean what they do they can forget or remember what they do but the human mind no the human mind has nothing to do with age.
> As I say so tears come into my eyes.[24]

Keith Waldrop

Notes

1. Richard Bridgman, *Gertrude Stein in Pieces* (N.Y.: Oxford, 1970), pp. 151-154.

2. Gertrude Stein, *Lectures in America* (Boston: Beacon, 1957— first published in 1935), p. 145. Cf. "the rhythm of anybody's personality" (p. 174).

3. Gertrude Stein, *Selected Writings*, ed. Carl Van Vechten (N.Y.: Modern Library, 1962), p. 434.

4. Gertrude Stein, *The Making of Americans* (N.Y.: Something Else Press, 1965—a photographic reprint of the first [1925] edition), p. 154.

5. *Selected Writings*, p. 329.

6. *Selected Writings*, p. 550.

7. *Selected Writings*, p. 477.

8. *Lectures in America*, p. 119. Here is the last act of "What Happened":

ACT V

(Two)

"A regret a single regret makes a door way. What is a door way, a door way is a photograph. What is a photograph a photograph is a sight and a sight is always a sight of something. Very likely there is a photograph that gives color if there is then there is that color that does not change any more than it did when there was much more use for photography" *(Selected Writings*, p. 560).

9. Bridgman, p. 121.

10. *Lectures in America*, pp. 191-92.

11. Lev Semenovich Vygotsky, *Thought and Language*, trans. Eugenia Hanfmann & Gertrude Vakar (Cambridge: MIT, 1962), p. 131. The original was published, posthumously, in 1934. I am not, of course, suggesting that Stein had any knowledge of this book.

12. Vygotsky, p. 15.

13. Vygotsky, p. 139.

14. *Lectures in America*, p. 210. It might be noted that Vygotsky also makes the connection between inner speech and lovers' talk,

taking his example from *Anna Karenina* (Vygotsky, pp. 139-141).

15. Gertrude Stein, *Geography and Plays* (Boston: Four Seas, 1922), p. 201. For an analysis of this portrait, see Wendy Steiner, *Exact Resemblance to Exact Resemblance* (New Haven: Yale University Press, 1978) pp. 83-89.

16. Vygotsky, pp. 146-47. Kandinsky, writing in 1910—knowing nothing of Stein's work—seems appropriate here: "The apt use of a word (in its poetical sense), its repetition, twice, three times, or even more frequently, according to the need of the poem, will not only tend to intensify the internal structure but also bring out unsuspected spiritual properties in the word itself. Further, frequent repetition of a word (a favorite game of children, forgotten in later life) deprives the word of its external reference. Similarly, the symbolic reference of a designated object tends to be forgotten and only the sound is retained. We hear this pure sound, unconsciously perhaps, in relation to the concrete or immaterial object. But in the latter case pure sound exercises a direct impression on the soul. The soul attains to an objectless vibration, even more complicated, I might say more transcendent, than the reverberations released by the sound of a bell, a stringed instrument, or a fallen board. In this direction lie great possibilities for the literature of the future." (Wassily Kandinsky, *Concerning the Spiritual in Art* [N.Y.: George Wittenborn, 1947], p. 34)

17. Vygotsky, p. 145.

18. *Lectures in America*, p. 122.

19. *Lectures in America*, p. 160.

20. *Lectures in America*, p. 169.

21. *Lectures in America*, p. 53.

22. Quoted by Michael J. Hoffman in *The Development of Abstractionism in the Writings of Gertrude Stein* (Philadelphia: University of Pennsylvania Press, l965), p. 154(n).

23. *Narration: Four Lectures* (Chicago: University of Chicago Press, 1969—first published in 1935), p. 15.

24. N.Y.: Vintage, 1973—first published in 1936, p. 63.

Introducing

One was a completely young one and this one was very clearly understanding this thing, clearly understanding that this one was a young one then and this one was one very clearly explaining this thing to every one and some indeed quite a number listened to him then and some of those listening were young ones then and some of those listening then were not young ones then.

The one who was completely a young one was one certainly very clearly then understanding this thing and quite clearly explaining this thing and explaining this thing clearly and quite often.

This one was one who was doing something and another thing and another thing and in a way he was doing each thing in the same way as he was doing each other thing and in a way there were differences and in a way certainly there were not any differences at all. He was a young one and he was clearly understanding this thing and he was certainly often very clearly explaining this thing. He was doing something and he certainly did it for sometime and it was certainly something he should then be doing. Some one might be thinking that he might be more successfully than doing some other thing but really not any one thought he should not be doing the thing he was doing when he was doing the thing and certainly he was very steadily doing the thing, the thing he was doing when he was doing that thing. In a way he had been doing a number of things, in a way he was always doing the same thing. He was a young one and he was completely clearly understanding this thing and he was completely when he was explaining this thing completely clearly explaining this thing.

He certainly was understanding something. He certainly was understanding and clearly explaining being a young one in his being a young one. Certainly he was listening and listening very often. Certainly he was understanding something, he was clearly understanding his being then a young one. He certainly was listening very much and very often. He certainly was sometimes explaining something. He certainly was clearly explaining his being a young one, he certainly was clearly understanding and clearly explaining this thing.

He could certainly pretty clearly ask what was the meaning of anything he was hearing. He certainly could ask quite clearly what was the way that something could come to have the meaning that thing had in being existing. He could almost completely clearly ask about something that some one had been explaining. He could completely clearly ask a question, he could almost completely clearly then ask another question, he could not quite completely clearly ask another question about that thing, he certainly could not completely clearly ask a question then again, ask another question then. He could certainly completely clearly explain being a young one in being then a young one, he certainly could completely clearly explain this thing, he certainly could completely clearly understand this thing.

He certainly did do a thing and go on sometime and go on and steadily go on doing that thing and certainly he did begin getting to explain quite clearly why he was doing that thing, what he was doing then, what he was not doing then. Certainly he did then explain quite clearly about his doing that thing and he was then certainly completely steadily doing that thing. He was quite steadily doing that thing, he certainly was quite completely then understanding his doing that thing, he certainly was very steadily doing that thing. He certainly was very steadily doing another thing then, he certainly quite completely understood his doing that thing then, he certainly quite completely and clearly understood his doing that thing then. He certainly did that thing very steadily then. He certainly quite completely clearly understood his doing that thing then. He certainly did another thing then, he certainly quite steadily quite entirely steadily did that thing then. He certainly quite clearly understood his doing that thing then. He certainly very steadily did that thing then. He certainly quite completely understood his doing that thing then. He certainly did another thing then. He certainly very steadily did that thing then. He certainly quite completely, he certainly quite clearly understood his doing that thing then.

He certainly did listen and listen again and again, he certainly quite steadily did this thing. He certainly quite clearly asked a question then. He certainly did sometimes quite clearly ask another question then. He did certainly sometimes did and quite clearly ask another question then, and certainly then he commenced listening again and he went on then listening and he continued then being listening.

He certainly was not ever about the same thing asking the same question again. He certainly was listening again to the same thing, he certainly was not asking the same question about the same thing again. In a way then he was not one asking the same questions again and again. He certainly was not asking the same question about the same thing and he certainly was one understanding clearly his being a young one and he certainly was quite often quite clearly explaining this thing and he was doing something and he was completely steadily doing that thing and he was completely clearly understanding his doing that thing. He certainly did amuse some and he certainly did interest some and he certainly did not disappoint some and he certainly did go on being living and certainly he did quite clearly understand being a young one in being a young one and he certainly did very nearly completely clearly and quite often explain this thing to some who were and to some who were then not themselves then young.

1.

Farragut or A Husband's Recompense

In anticipation.
Baking.
This is breathing.
Neglected.
What.
Half.

In anticipation.
Caesar drinking.
What.
Hear.
In anticipation hearing what, hear.

In anticipation.
What happened.
When.
In the year 1877 when there was a resolution there was quicker travelling. It was listening then and jealous feeling. On the part of whom.
Listening.
They came to bathe that day.
Any day was the principal day. Every day was beside it beside that circumstance the circumstance that kept it absolutely evaded.
Oh dear.
Farragut.

At home in Italy.
Why were they at home in Italy. Because of here.

Why were they at home in Italy. Because the youngest was three years old. Tall. Blessed and useful.

What could they do. They didn't leave it.

It came then. What.

Stretching.

Stretching what.

Stretching everything.

For what.

For returning.

Where did they return.

They did not return.

Anyway.

How do you do.

Very well I thank you.

Early years.

Not alone oh no not alone. Not visited. By this blessing. They wouldn't have been useful. They wouldn't have been useful but they would have been necessary. It was necessary that they should be together by shoes.

They came to raffle this later. Not really. It was very hard to lose their mother-in-law.

Hard.

Almost impossible.

Earlier years.

I really ought not to bake apples and seed raisins and have fowls and be bewildered. I really ought to smile. I can remember how astonishing it was to be so actively sweet that I promised to see a lemon orchard. I remember it very well.

We put them all into cigar boxes.

We have no way of being surprised.

Dictionaries were not a surprise.

I don't believe there was any water. If there had been why didn't we go swimming together. I don't believe either that

6

there was any sun. Grass had that way about it and afterwards when the wind blew I knew I was a protection. What did I protect I protected icing. In what way was there icing. There was icing because there was indivisible union. I don't want any remarks. I have a selfish way of saying, tell me how I love you.
Grammar.
Grammar was a festival.
So was spelling.
So was permission.
So was it all.
I have started permission.
Please be neat.
Please be complete.
Please guess fingers.
Which is it.
The fourth.
Which is it now.
The first.
Which is it now.
The third.
Which is it now.
The little one.
Now you guess.
Which is it now.
The third.
No the fourth.
Which is it now.
The second.
No the fourth.
Which is it now.
The third.
No the fourth.

Which is it now.
The fourth.
No the third.
Which is it now.
I don't want to guess any more.
Recently there was a change in furniture. The leading diffi-
culty had always been that in sitting there was no recog-
nition of clarification of clarification of sliding. This did
not seem an instance of the era of good feeling.
I want to know now how often it had been neces-
sary to copy all the special ways of sitting. I want to
know how obliging every one is. This has nothing to do
with us.
                    Crossing.
What was crossing.
The boat.
Where was it going.
It wasn't going it was coming.
When did it come.
It came on time.
When it came there did not happen to be there any one to
meet it. This was not an oversight. This was not negligence,
it was not meant to show slight, it was not meant to be care-
less. It made meeting exciting. Exciting to whom. Exciting
to those being ones being exciting.
I was naughty.
To whom.
I was there.
When.
When I was there.
I was there all the time.
When was I there.
I was there when I was there.

I was there all the time.
When was I there.
I was there all the time.
I was there all the time.
The first thing I saw was an explosion. An explosion of what of retaliation.
There was no need to question. Every one was pleased.
Two bits worth of birthday.
I was born at eight o'clock.
This morning when I woke up it was I made that mistake it was eight o'clock.
Were you pleased.
I was.
I am now going to begin telling everything.
Shoving.
What is shoving.
It is not the expression of opinion.
It is not lightning.
It did not happen at first.
Just at first there was a dispute. Should one wait when one said one was waiting. Should one say one was waiting. Would it seriously threaten any one to be cowardly to offer to write and say something. Was it careless of a friend to insist on selecting what was powerless to influence. I wish I had a handkerchief.
This is entirely a different manner.
Shouting.
What is shouting.
It is a disease. Is there any way to stop it. There is a way and that way was the way that was shown to be their way. Dear things.
Leave it to me to explain what happened.
I can't remember the detail. The first that I can remember

is asking do you mean to deny that you heard me. I asked that often. The next thing that I remember is asking were you nervous again. The next thing that I can undertake to be remembering is were you flattering. Were you flattering me by voicing an objection. If so don't bother.

I don't really mean to be a slave.

In the morning I don't really mean in the morning.

What is penetrating.

Plants are penetrating.

I am going to be happy in winter.

So it's natural is it. Well it's quite what it should it should be natural and it is natural and that doesn't interfere with it in any way in respect to its being great literature.

Naturalness. What is naturalness, it is suggesting that pearls are shouting and treasures are kissing and ears are engaging and roses are prominent and eyes are speckled and foreheads are soft and hair is massive and a chin makes a whole. A whole what, a whole recreation.

I say I wished that I was there and I was there. I say I wish I was here and I am here.

I say that I shouted.

I say that I offered odours. I say that special sights are special sights.

What are powerful oats.

When she came there was grain.

I misjudged her, I said I could never picture her physical presence. I said I thought she had gone to see a plaster house. She hadn't. She hadn't been anywhere. She had just come. The first time I saw her was the day we met, by that I mean they were sitting, where were they sitting, they were sitting by their side. I don't mean to be foolish.

Suddenly I remembered. It was clear. It was quite clear. Did it do that. I asked some one. He said that it had been that way, that he had experienced everything, that fog was penetrating and moisture was lonesome and darkness was appalling. I said I didn't believe it.

What is success.

Success is what she was supposed to favour. How was she supposed to favour success. She was supposed to favour success by being fond of money. Whatever she said was earnest and thoughtful and showed rare decision. By that I mean Monkey. Monkey see monkey do. Monkey do what. Monkey loves me.

I stopped it. I said not so sweet. I did think I had that responsibility. I knew a better way to be a fourth way. I said didn't Henry and Herbert love you.

I will never be better again. Surely surely I shouldn't wonder.

Principal parts.

All parts are principal parts. Birthdays are saints days.

Does any one know when. By this yes. That winters and summers and some days all days are refreshing. Does any one know when why is it. By this means we conquer.

I don't think you can say this is too natural.

To go on with my story, by the time we were settled well we didn't settle easily, we had to decide what rights were willing. Were they willing, well I guess yes. This is the way it happened. Where shall I put my shoes. Where shall I put my shoes. Don't repeat it.

Where shall I put my shoes. I didn't expect you to put your shoes. Where shall I put my shoes. I don't think it's at all funny. I don't think I am willing to put my shoes where I am not to put them and I don't think that I will wait. I will put my shoes among shoes. Some call them boots. By this I mean that little ways have an end. They will be changed. By this I mean that little ways have an end. They will be changed. They will see to that and by this time I conquer.

So then accrediting moving.

I don't like rain. I don't mean that thunder scares me. You know very well what I mean I mean that sometimes I wish I was a fish with a settled smelling center. I don't like it. I think it's an ugly word.

How well I remember the quarrel. I don't often mention such things. They never can happen. But once it was very suddenly authentic.

I learned to say doesn't it fatigue you. I learned not to be ceremonious. I learned correct snatches.

Sometimes when it was warm, I came suddenly, I came suddenly to be there and to be exciting. It was worse than money.

Alright I will be natural.

B is for birthday baby and blessed.

S is for sweetie sweetie and sweetie.

Y is for you and u is for me and we are as happy as happy can be.

Returning to mutton that is to say to mention reforming. What a cake. What a kindness. What a smell. What a shame. What a slight. What a sound. What a universal shudder. I will not be coerced. But I was. Was I. I was coerced. I see it.

I began by saying that I had plenty of time and that I knew best. I said more things Sunday. Not Sunday to-day.

Perhaps that is too natural. The emphasis can be where you like.

If you had read the word the other way I wouldn't have minded.

I have forgotten what was mentioned.

A scene I remember very clearly was when we were coming

home and we had no time to settle what we would tell was the reason that we were expected. No I don't like spending my time saying that we were so slovenly.

Reading.

Is reading painful.

When one has not the habit of reading reading is not painful. One can read hands, one cannot compare that with reading a book. Either the one or the other is useful and both are so pleasing to the ear and eye.

I have the eye but not the hand of an artist.

Calling out loud. Were you worried when they decided that silver was Italian. I knew jolly well that you weren't and it was foolish to leave me and hear it. Italian was silver of course Italian was silver. I mean that it was a wonderful resemblance. One morning and the evening before I argued with leaning very well, I argued about reverberating, I argued about pealing, I argued about challenges and repetitions and sorrows and shawls and lined leather coats and parts of examples and repeated leopards and collars and astonishing reasons. I argued before.

I remember a feather. I don't mean the three, I couldn't remember no I couldn't remember how beautiful and curlily the rose feather and the shape to a feather could come together. A shape to a feather can come together. Violets and salt water.

Two and three quarters, two and a quarter two and a half.

Two and three quarters, two and a half two and a half.

Two and a half, two, two.

Two and a half one and a half one and a half.

I don't know the other.

Please be with me.

Black lines and sun make a change of night gear.

We went and bought flannel.

There is a slight difference only it is very difficult.
They were friends of him.
They were friends of him.
If possession means importance. They were friends for him.
They were friends of him.
His means holding it.
Two were friends of him.
I wrote it on blue paper to remind him of the blue vase.
This is serious.
I have to think.
To-night when we were sitting there I was asked if I meant to continue as I had been continuing or if I meant to commence again. Did I answer.
Whispering by command.
I can't remember all of it.
The first day that Leonard went away it was very considerate of him. I remember all about sleeping. I remember all about awaking. I remember thinking do we mean to be serious. Do we mean to idolise. Do we secrete anything. I remember thinking and not being vague. Resolution is not formidable. Then it was rather absurd of us to tell some one that she must do it she must do it she must do it. The thing that I remember that was most amusing and most learned was that there were pins for us all. Dear pins. How easily we were pleased.
It isn't difficult to please us.
Fourteen.
Fourteen.
Roses.
When I was wishing and sitting I wished for a clock. I meant to pick out an expensive one. I did so and now dear one is economising. That isn't right. I meant it is right. I mean it is right for bathing in one. It is right to be econo-

mising. It is right for dear one to be economising. And some day we will be rich. You'll see. It won't be a legacy, it won't be selling anything, it won't be purchasing, it will just be irresistible and then we will spend money and buy everything a dog a Ford letter paper, furs, a hat, kinds of purses, and nearly something new that we have not yet been careful about. This is natural. Very natural.

We won't keep any letters of Frank's .

I remember another thing. We were walking and all of a sudden there was oiling, I mean a little oil was forming, it had formed on the chin. I had been told that there was something and I was suspicious of this thing and I was mistaken.

I said go home if you like.

I said I was an authority.

I said I could be angry.

I said nothing.

We went on terrorising.

Then we came to a hill.

We settled on the hill.

I said is it likely that I am stubborn.

An answer.

Not such as would be given.

There came to be then a time when answering was everything. Yes. When saying, I am going to speak first, is nothing.

It has no success.

It isn't shattering.

Please prepare me.

I want to be lovely and then. I want to be lively and then. I want to be lively and then I say isn't it fortunate that we were early, that I was severe that I meant all I said. I want to be early and lively. I want to be especially adapted. I am

clean and concise and I estimate everything at their value.
I am not in a hurry.
It was natural.
Mike said they ate themselves up.
It was natural
It is natural to me.
Look
At
Me
I can read that we are all fat.
We are the lovely pair of.
I remember that we came to stay at the place where water
was drunk. We all said it was necessary. It was a mistake.
We drove her to it but I will not mention another one.
Finally.
Finely.
Finally we had an unpleasant time about the letters. We
were all mistaken. It wasn't true at all.
I made that wish.
When we went to Spain we never expected to hear about
Italy.
It was not a surprise.

PART TWO

How Farragut Reformed Her and How She Reformed Him. "Oh that frightens me."

I like it.

I am not complaining.

The whole title of the second part is. They don't frighten me. Yes they do though. We don't have to go right on we wait until inspiration overtakes us. You are so distinguished. I'll go on both sides hereafter. Indeed you ought to I should say.

Which is rather out of the way period.

Dearest, supposing you tell me that you love me.

I don't know whether it's a door, or up there or the window. I don't know whether it's up there.

I want to know about reform. This is the way it comes about. You ask for stages. You say can you remember this. You say tell me everything everybody says. You say don't be envious.

Then you go on and puzzle.

Then you delight in marshes. Then you receive countenances. And then you look whether you are graceful or not.

By that time many thin sands make glass. Many thin sands make glass.

I know now. It isn't that.

It wasn't next time.

Don't be stupid.

Don't sing.

That was a chance.

I don't care anything about it.

Please be careful.

I don't like to be thorough. I like to come down in the morning and wake and then supper. I don't mean everyday. Regularly.

This is not about me.

Pardon me, did you hear.

I want it to be natural. I want it to tell about reform and how changed reform is and how questions can be asked.

I am not frightened by cows. Anyway.

That's a good thing to talk about, apples. Apples and cows. All of it. Apples cows, apples cows. Apple Cows. I don't mean that way. Anybody knows the expense.

I thought she meant splitting. Not spitting.

I don't believe it.

I have faith.

We were formerly.

We are winsome.

A husband's recompense is to have his wife so Farragut finishes.

2.

Wherein the South Differs from the North

An agreement in it.
As the north.
As the north in agreement with it.
Are they ready yet.
Not yet.
In the north in agreement with it.
North in agreement with it.
North is a name all the same.
North in agreement with it.
And the north in agreement with it.
As the South in an agreement with it.
And an agreement with the South.
South is not a name.
And the same.
The south is not a name.
And in the same way the south is not in agreement. An in
agreement. An agreement. And an agreement. As an agree-
ment. The South is not in agreement with it.
Not as useful it is not as useful.
Used to used to, used to the same used to it and used to the
same. Used to it used to the same. To see the same. Used to
see the same. Used to the same.
North used to the same. The north used to see the same.
The north used to see the same, the north used to see the
same the north used to used to see the same.
The north used to see the same.

Or the south. The south or the south or the south did did the south ordinarily the south ordinarily did do did it usefully. It did it usefully. The south ordinarily did it usefully. As fat as that.

In this way.

North has north what has north thought about it.

And in this way.

What has the north and what has the north what has the north finished. What has that made what has made that, what is made and what is it that it has made. It has made the fact that in this way not only is there an interruption and no interruption recedes not only has there been no interruption but as to being careful, carefully now.

And so forth.

It is perfectly useless to entertain.

So much so much so much.

It is why to change, it is why it is necessary to change. It is in change.

Numbers do it.

North and south negroes.

No one means that.

South and north settle.

No one means that.

No one means that south and north settle, South and north settle no one means that.

Furthermore.

What would it do, how would it do, would it do as it is.

It is a very extraordinary phenomena, that it has always been a habit to remark that seasons have ceased to exist and in this way it is the intention to express that seasons have lost their identity.

Not at all in this way.

A pleasure.

Baby pearls.
S for south and n for north s and n for south and north.
No not kneeling.
It is certainly a conclusion which has been come to that there is no reason why if in the midst of the two in their midst, if in their midst if in their midst, collectively. As many.
North water, south water, south water, north water. No difference.
All at once as soon, all at once so soon all at once and all at once and all at once and soon. To say so soon. Can ask.
They can ask which way they can go. They can ask and they can ask if they can ask.
An interruption and in between.
As an interruption can it be different.
As an interruption can it be differently.
And as an interruption.
North as an interruption.
The north as an interruption. It did not interrupt.
As in interruption. The North was not interrupted. North was not interrupted. Uninterrupted. Not interrupted. Uninterrupted. As uninterrupted as the south. As uninterrupted as North is uninterrupted as South is uninterrupted as north and south and as uninterrupted. Nobody shares pears.
The second time.
Too busy to say so.
First along.
Dislike choosing.
Second along.
Going to choose.
First choice.
North.

Second choice.
South.
Third choice
South.
Fourth choice.
North.
First choice.
North.
Second choice.
South.
Third choice.
South.
Fourth choice.
North.
Fourth choice and first choice.
North.
Third choice and second choice.
South.
Second choice.
South.
Third choice.
South.
Fourth choice.
North.
First choice.
North.
First choice.
North.
First choice.
North.
First choice.
North.
First choice and fourth choice.

North.
Third choice and second choice.
South.
Third choice and second choice.
Fourth choice and first choice.
First choice and fourth choice and second choice and third choice.
South and north.
Next.
South and north.
To dislike sending.
To dislike sending it.
To dislike sending it there.
Where.
Partly north.
Partly north and partly north.
Not partly south.
Partly north and not partly south.
No more capital. Capitals are so worth while.
North what north. What north. What north and which North. Which is north. Which is north. Where is north.
Where is the north. North of it.
North of it. The north a north, it is north it is north of the south it is as south of the north it is as south it is as south of the north. It is as south of the north as that.
When it is anticipated, when they are anticipated, when they anticipate what is to happen as if it were to be arranged and more often indeed made responsible for it, if it is equally and gradually if they are gradually persuaded that they need not and they have to be they have not to be refused then in that case there is no need for opposition. Candidly say so. And so forth.

More than opinion. More than that opinion. And more than that as that opinion. To say so.

Refusing and under and under refusing and refusing and under refusing have it and have it so and to have it so.

One and two, sound as around as around as round as the well and as very well. Very well sir.

The North shall be satisfied and the South also.

All the elements of an introduction and now to proceed to debate. A debate does mean that as antedate and as rebate and as restate and as rightfully as they can.

The first martyr.

Martyrology as understood.

How suddenly they succeed one another and as suddenly.

As at first a martyr.

As at first a martyr all the time.

As at first a martyr.

The martyr.

Martyrology understood and carefully annotated as ob-served and not withdrawn from.

May we if we please.

Not as north as as south.

Not as north.

Now north.

Acceptably.

Cunningly say so.

They cunningly said so.

As nice and so forth.

They led them to it.

They led them away from it.

As nice and so forth.

As the north.

As nice and so forth.

Believe them and so forth.

And believe them and and believe them.

If when and more nearly fairly well nearly very well, very well nearly accustomed to coming as they had formerly energetically countenanced exchanging, exchanging bundles for bundles. Not at all. Not exchanging bundles for bundles. Why not at all. Why not at all why not at all because if new since is more nearly replaced not every day but methods, supposing for instance that there are preparations, preparations enough.

Think it is right, and necessary. Think it is necessary. They think it is necessary as that.

What do you think.

What do you think what do you think when each one has a name. Do you think that it indicates the place a place. Place it.

Do they think do they think in case of. North. Go north. South. As south.

Do they think do they think in case of it. In case of it do they think. Prepare to astonish everybody.

Make it more north than south do make it more north than south to make it more north than south, make it north and make it south. Up or down, down or up, as up or up, up or down or up. Europe.

Not covered up as much or much, not covered or as much or much. Much covered up, much covered or much covered up. Is it much covered up.

North and south needlessly.

North and south considerably and for this, this makes it. North. This makes it north as much as south. This makes it south as much as north. A struggle to say so. Say so. As say so. Could it be a custom to select fish because they are flatter than they were. Could it be a custom. Could they become accustomed to it. As much as that.

Not north.
Not the north.
Not too north.
Not easily south.
Not ordered south.
South and North mentioned the south and north mentioned.
North did you say.
And north did you say.
In that direction.
North did you say.
As north did you say.
As in that direction.
As you say.
When it is more nearly come again when is it more nearly and come again and south as south as that. Suppose you were used to it, suppose you meant by that something else, supposing in that specialty supposing as that reminded by it, reminded by it and reminded and not as she shuts it, shuts it, not as she shuts it. As she shuts it and reminded, remind her of it, to remind her that it is as that it is as particularly, it is particularly wanted, and remind to remind can remind how do you remind them that once in a while very much as that is. See there. It was changeable. See there it was changeable.
If at a time and a time is more if in time and in time to hear, if in the rest particularly scared, scared of it, afraid to say so, all the time any time and plentifully, currents plentifully, chances plenty of chances, extensively.
This breaks up a union.
Remember to get up. To remember and to remember and get up. Get up.
How many countries can you count.

Count count count.

How many countries can you have counted.

How many countries have you counted in this count.

How many countries have you counted.

North by north.

Counted.

Lost it up lost it as up, lost it up, happily lost it as up and lost it as up. You don't say so.

Lost it up. Lost it as up. And happily lost it as up. Lost it up.

Lost it as up.

That is done.

One run. Say so.

One run that is done say so.

Say so that is done one run that is done.

Not not hot.

Not not as what.

Not and not.

Not as hot.

Not as what.

Not.

North.

South.

Plenty of time.

North and south as we say plenty of time.

Not north for nothing.

Not for nothing.

Not north and not for nothing.

Not north and not for nothing. North not for nothing.

For nothing.

South for nothing.

Not South.

Not for the South and not for nothing.

Next.
Not next.
Not next to north.
Not annexed.
Not next to it.
And not next to it.
Next to it.
North and south for nothing.
Not deceived by the moon, not deceived and at noon not deceived very soon not deceived just as soon not deceived and not deceived any more.
Not deceived any more about the sun and Sunday she was not deceived any more about the sun and Sunday.
Not deceived any more she was not deceived any more in the north. Not deceived any more as to the north and as to the south not deceived any more as to the South and not deceived any more as to the south.
She was not deceived any more in the north she was not deceived any more as to the south.
Any more as to the South.
In the middle of attention.
Any more as to the north.
In the middle of inattention.
Any more as to the north.
Any more as to the north.
In the middle as an attention.
Any more as to the north.
In the middle as in attention.
Any more as to the north.
In the middle of an intention.
Any more as to the north.
And any more as to the north.
Settled is it.

Is it settled.
Settled is it.
In attention as to the south.
Settled is it.
In attention as to the north.
It is settled is.
In attention as to the south.
In attention in intention.
It is settled.
As to the south.
Come again come again.
Up.
Come again come again down.
Not so easily.
Come again come again up.
As come again up.
Feeling an attraction the or center center of course.
To please furnish to please and furnish to please and to
furnish, to please and to furnish and to furnish please.
North and south nestles.
North and south nestles north and south.
South and north nestles south and north.
South and north nestles.
South and north nestles south and north. And north and
south and south and north and not in as much. Nestles.
If it was meant that all the same when it was it came back
again.
Another instance.
He would and he would and he would and he would.
Around it.
Not around it.
If if if we, if if if they, if if if he if if if he if we if we
if he anyway, if he. So much so.

Plenty of violence.
Made of papers made of papers it is made of papers to be made of papers it is to be made of papers. It is to be made of paper. It is to be made of papers.
If if anyway. It is anyway. If it is anyway.
Was he big or was he.
He was large.
In there in the meantime.
A chance to notice.
Now a new way.
If in the meantime if and in the way and as they say, said.
In union there is strength.
Right and left.
No.
Left and right.
No.
Left and right.
No.
Right and left.
No.
Oh no.
Right and left.
Left and right.
No.
No.
Left and right.
Right and left.
No not right and left, no not left and right.
No not right and left.
Not left and right.
Left and right.
No.
Right and left.

No.

Not left and right.

Not right and left.

Other changes.

North as is best.

South as is best.

Not as is best.

North not as is best.

South not as is best.

Rid of it.

To be rid of it.

To be rid of it and not south.

To be rid of it.

To be rid of it and not so south. To be rid of it and not as south as to be rid of it as to be rid of it and not as south and not to be rid of it.

Many additions. There are as many additions to it as there were.

Coming in as before.

Are they coming as they were before. Yes and no and they say so, can say so and can say so.

Yes and no.

Instantly.

For instance.

A little observation as to the impression made upon one by observing the difference in the light and heat made by artificial light and the sun, also the difference made by the impression as to how it all had happened. And was he as satisfied, and was he, as he was satisfied. A little observation of the difference made by all the difference experienced as nearly as can be exactly. Not to be exactly careful. This can be taught.

Once more.

Restitution.

Bargains bear up bear up bargains, bargains and it is bargains. To bargain into the bargain.

Not only but also the explorer should be able to know how to and also to recognise the spots he has seen before and which he will recognise again as he occupies as he successively occupies as he occupies successively the places he recognises and not only that he occupies them successively but also that he will later be able to make maps of the region which he has traversed. Such is the duty of an explorer. In short it depends upon him in short he is to realise that he is to acquire knowledge of the directions of the direction of a direction of previous visits and successive visits. It becomes necessary therefor that he indulges in active plans and map drawing and also in constant observation and relative comparisons. In this way he easily finds his way.

Where is it is it there there it is. North there it is and there it is once more and yet and again, once more to resist attacking a new fashion of remodeling and so much more.

As so much more. Fancy it, fancy that a nuisance fancy that it is a nuisance. That it is a nuisance to consider that up and north and up and doing and up and south and up and doing and across and all of it. Expectantly shining, as is easier than that and not always fairly presentable. An entirely new type of ship and an entirely new type of ship and an entirely new type of ship.

Choose it. Choose it as carefully as the north choose it as carefully as the south choose it as carefully or the north choose it as carefully or the south or the south or the north or choose it as carefully.

Share and share, if a share of it if a share of it is there there where in the meantime all day long as it is. Joined immediately. It was joined immediately it was joined to it immediately.

When there is more or or less when there is more or less in the meantime when there is more or less when there is more or less in the meantime. In the meantime when there is more or less.

The north manages it very well, as the south manages it very well as the south manages it very well as the north manages it very well.

Ninety-two, as well as ninety-two.

Ready and ready enough and very ready and readily, readily stated stated intervals intervals come.

Come some, some come, come come, come some some some come. Intervals stated stated intervals, readily stated stated intervals and very readily, stated intervals as some come at stated intervals. Plant and planted. In the north planted and plant it in the south plant it and planted. In the north planted and plant it in the south plant it and planted. In the north in the south in the north planted in the south plant it in the south planted in the north plant it, plant it planted in the north planted in the south plant it in the north plant it in the north plant it. In the south planted, in the south planted, in the south planted in the south planted, in the south plant it in the north planted. Planted in the north. Next to it usually. Usually next to it. In the south usually next to it in the north usually next to it, in the the north usually in the south usually in the south usually in the north usually next to it in the south usually next to it in the north usually next to it in the south usually next to it, in the south usually next to it in the north usually next to it.

Does it was it was it does it does it go was it gone was it does it does it have was it far was it does it does it come was it

33

for it was it was it for it does it do it does it does it do it was it for it was it for it does it do it.

Was it as far was it as far as that, was it was it as far as that and was it.

To to be too to be to be north to be north to be north to be south to be south to be north to be to be south to be it is to be north it is to be it is to be south it is to be south and north it is to be north and south. It is to be.

The rush south was over as the rush south was over. The rush north was over or the rush north was over. Over and over. As the rush north was over as the rush south was over the rush north and the rush south were over.

Plenty of instances are needed to explain that if in the interests of telling in the interest of telling this is told there are plenty of instances of this being told to explain that in the interests that in those interests in the interest it is in their interest it is to the interest of the north that it is told it is because it is to the best interests of the south that it is told it is told to explain the best interests that there are interests that there is interest in the north that there is this interest in the south that there is interest for the south that there is interest that there is enough interest to interest the north and that there is enough to interest the south just enough to interest and enough explanation of the interest and of the south and enough explanation of the north and enough interest. There enough interest.

North and south expected, north and south it is expected, north and south expected, expected, north and south, expected. Expect, what to expect. Expected what is it that is expected. North and south expected, what is expected north and south expect, expect north and south. To expect north and south, to expect, expected, expected north and south, expect north and south expect. Expect north and south.

Next time.

Expect north and south next time. Next time expected north and south. Expected north and south next time.

What is seen in between in between as the north in between what is seen what is seen in between. What is it what is seen in between what is it. What is it what is seen in between. What is seen in between the south what is seen, what is it what is seen in between. In between has the reason, flowers please as much as gloves, gloves do not please any more. Gloves please flowers please if you please. As much as gloves if you please. Not any more if you please. Please as please. What is it. And so as it is nearly as much of an advantage as ever.

North north it, it is not an advantage as it were. South south by it it is not an advantage as it were. As if it were, as if it were as an assembly.

Mainly able meanly able to mainly able to put through mainly able to go through mainly able to go through to the north mainly able to go through to mainly able also to go through to the south and to the north. Mainly able to.

Stretches and stretches if it stretches as it stretches as stretches. Stretches and stretches.

Mainly able to as it stretches toward the south mainly able to and it stretches to the north. As it stretches mainly able to go through to the south as south. Mainly able to. As many as are able to as much as there is to do.

As much as there is to do just as much as there is to do, to do just as much as there is to do, to do, just as much, to do just as much, to do, just as much, as there is, to do just as much as there is, to do, just as much, as there is, to do, to do, just, to do just as much, to do just as much as there is, to do just as much as there is to do.

Have it as we have it. An authority, formerly and favourable as favourable as that.

Two makes two two makes two too, two makes too as for instance. Two makes too, nicely. Two makes too, two and two and nicely. Two makes too nicely.

It happened again as it happened again as it happened again and sustained too as it happened again and it was sustained too as it happened again. As it happened again, when, as it happened again and was sustained too. Fairly speaking. Find it up find it up, find it up and find it up. All up. Find it all up, find it all up and find it up. Up as up, upper as upper, find it up, finding if finding find and upper makes a difference, it does not matter very much. Very much a difference upper finding up, finding out, if it makes very much difference if it makes a difference and more so in the case as constituted. It is very likely to be very well arranged. Very well arranged.

In plenty of time there can be, in plenty of time they can be there in plenty of time, they can be there they can be there in plenty of time. They can be there in plenty of time and not as well as they all know it. As well as they all know it and there is no effort in it. There is no effort for it and as well as they all know it. And as well as they all know it and there is no effort in it. There is an effort for it and as well as they all know it. And as well as they all know it and there is an effort for it. There is an effort for it and as well as they all know it.

As well as they all know it would if it could would if it could be avoided would it if it could be avoided would it be if it could be avoided. And north. North of it. Would it if it could be avoided would it south of it. Would it north of it. Would it south of it. Would it if it could be avoided north of it. Would it if it could be avoided south of it. Would it if it could be avoided south of it in the meantime. Would it if it could be avoided in the meantime north of it. Would it if it could be avoided in the meantime north of it. Would it north of it in the meantime would it if it could be avoided in the meantime would it in the meantime north of it would it in the meantime if it could be avoided south of it. In the meantime.

Plenty of plants there are plenty of plants planted here and there those plants. There are plenty of those plants planted. North here and there. South here and there. Planted here and there. Come to Mary, a name. North a name come to Mary. North. Come to Mary. South. A name. Here and there. Come to Mary. South. A name. Come to Mary. South here and there a name. Come to Mary here and there a name. North here and there a name. North, Mary here and there a name. Here and there a name south, Mary here and there a name. Here and there a name Mary, north, here and there a name. Here and there a name Mary. Here and there a name. Here and there a name Mary a name. Here and there a name North a name. Here and there Mary a name. Here and there Mary a name South a name. Here and there a name North a name. Here and there a name south a name. Here and there a name.

3.

Wherein Iowa Differs from Kansas and Indiana

Otherwise seen and otherwise see and otherwise seen to see, to see otherwise.

Otherwise seen. The difference to be seen the difference and otherwise seen, the difference and otherwise seen the difference seen otherwise.

In Iowa, in there, in Iowa and in there in there and in Iowa it is noticeable the difference in there the difference in Iowa and in there.

Iowa means much.

Much much much.

For so much.

Iowa means much.

Indiana means more.

More more more.

Indiana means more. As more.

Kansas means most and most and most and most. Kansas means most merely.

This is the difference between those three.

Samples.

Have examples.

Add examples.

Added examples.

Every one has heard it said.

Iowa in Iowa and in Iowa no one had heard it said in Iowa.

In Indiana and in Indiana and they heard it said in Indiana.

In Iowa heard it said in Iowa.

In Indiana and heard it said.

In Kansas and in Kansas how it was heard how it was said how it was heard and said and in Kansas how was it heard as said.

And in Iowa held it.

And in Kansas hold it so as to hold it for it. In Indiana held it to hold it, hold it to hold it. In Iowa held it, in Kansas hold it, in Indiana to hold it.

Do you see what I mean.

As a question.

A question is made to state something that has not been replied to there.

Is Iowa up or down.

Is Indiana down and why.

Is Kansas up and down and where is it.

There are questions only because no one thinks of three things at one time.

Iowa plans for Iowa these are not the plans for Iowa.

Kansas and Indiana the plans for Kansas and Indiana are these.

There are the plans for Indiana.

Iowa for four more for four more and four more. Iowa for more. For more and Iowa. Changed four to for, changed for to four.

Indiana four. Indiana for.

For Kansas.

Fortunately for and as fortunately for and fortunately for Iowa.

Indiana and four and leave it alone and all.

Kansas and not to leave it all alone and so forth.

Iowa and so forth.

Iowa evidences, there are evidences that Iowa, there is

evidence that in Iowa or in evidence, for instance as an instance and in Iowa.

More than an instance and in evidence and in Indiana and for instance. The instance and as evidence and Indiana and evident and as Indiana and as evident.

And Kansas and as evident and as an instance and for instance and in Kansas for instance and as evident as Kansas and as evident and as an instance and as for instance and as for instance for instance as Kansas and as for instance next to it.

As next to it nearly as next to it nearly in Iowa next to it.

In Indiana for four more next to it four more next to it and Indiana and Indiana for four.

In Kansas and not next to it and so so.

Next foremost and a plan, a plan and next to it and foremost foremost and next to it and a plan and planned as planned as foremost and next to it and a plan. Consider Iowa as considerably as so.

In Indiana next to it and foremost and a plan and also and foremost and also and consider it and also and as considerably and also as Indiana and foremost and considerably and also and next to it, and next to it and also and considerably and foremost and a plan and next to it and foremost and considerably and also, and also and considerably and plan it and next to it and considerably. And Kansas and considerably and also and foremost, and foremost and considerably and also and also and Kansas and considerably and foremost and also and Kansas and a plan and Kansas and considerably and Kansas and foremost and Kansas and next to it and foremost and Kansas and considerably and foremost and Kansas and a plan and Kansas and considerably.

Iowa and not another difference, Indiana and if and not if

another difference and if another difference if a difference if a difference in Kansas, if Kansas is different.

If Iowa or so if Iowa has if Iowa has had if Iowa has to have, if Iowa is to have to have, and if in Indiana and if it has to have if Indiana has to have it and if Kansas has had has to have has it, if Iowa Indiana Kansas if Kansas Iowa Indiana, if Indiana Kansas Iowa has it has it, if Iowa has it if Kansas has it if Indiana has it has to have it had it, if Iowa had it, if Kansas had to have it or what nest.

Not continued as Iowa, not continued as as continued as Iowa, as continued Iowa as continued and Indiana as continued as Indiana and as Kansas as Kansas as continued.

The next makes a meeting between Iowa, to notice, the next makes a meeting between Indiana a notice the next makes a meeting between Kansas or makes a between Kansas or makes a meeting, Indiana makes a meeting, Iowa a meeting, Iowa a meeting, makes a meeting Indiana, makes a meeting Kansas. Meeting Kansas meeting Indiana meeting Iowa, next meeting Iowa next meeting Indiana next meeting Kansas.

Next.

Meeting.

Next meeting as if they had to have parties Kansas, as if they had to have parties. Indiana and as if they had parties as if that had to have parties and Iowa has to have a part and parties.

Iowa Iowa and this to see Iowa Iowa in a little while, formally. Iowa Iowa and next and next Iowa Iowa in a minute. So much for that. Indiana as Indiana or outwardly more so Indiana for Indiana more than a half, Indiana in the meantime reflected again. As for Kansas purely as for Kansas surely as for Kansas hourly as for Kansas, as for Kansas hourly as for Kansas as for Kansas fairly as for

Kansas and as for Kansas, for favourably as for Kansas for for it.

Iowa forty-four Indiana forty-four fifty, Kansas fifty-four forty and so forth.

Iowa has made it, Indiana has it and has it made it, Kansas and has it made it as it has it.

Iowa for fourteen, Iowa four fourteen, Indiana fourteen, fourteen for all, Kansas as fourteen are four more than ten exactly.

The next question has an answer.

Iowa and the next question has an answer.

Indiana has the next question and has the next answer.

Kansas question and answer.

Has the next question an answer, is the answer is this answer is this the answer to the next question.

The next question and the next answer.

The next question.

Iowa and the next question.

Indiana and the next question.

Iowa and the next question.

Indiana and the next question. Iowa and the next question or the next question or Iowa. Indiana and the next question and the next question Indiana and the next question, the next question left the next question Kansas and the next question, Indiana Iowa Kansas and the next question.

4.

The Difference Between the Inhabitants of France and the Inhabitants of the United States of America

There is a difference between France and the United States of America in the character of their inhabitants. There is this difference between France and the United States of America in the character of its inhabitants. The inhabitants of the United States of America have this quality in their character in reference to drama that the things they do and the thing that they do do are such things that when they are young are different than when they are older. For instance when they are young and violent, then when they are young and then when they are violent and when they are not young and when they are not young are they not young and not as violent. Drama consists and in this they are so they are so certainly restricted, restricted to that themselves and not any more so. Thank you is not mentioned. In France especially so and for this reason especially when they are young and as an example not at all exacting not at all as exacting and when they are young and not any more so not feverishly so not as exacting exactly and as an instance and in collusion and not in very nearly as many cases secondary. The need of thanking for this is taught by description.

Five examples of each will be given.

Five examples of each will be given so that the difference will be as well understood as ever. As ever and so much and so forth for nearly and very nearly all the same in a minute and as connected for it is as it shall should or may be yes. May be it may be as yes as yes so there and so there would have been some noise to-day.

In the beginning did she know her that is to say as she was away from home and as she was away from home did she know her. This makes fountains remain with her too with her too. No one need decide whether it is or is not used by the ones sending or whether in order that the ones sending are able to send whether it is necessary to send then beforehand a written address arranged in the fashion that is habitual and expected by the employees who will have to handle it in the ordinary course of the arrangement. And a letter follows when an envelope and a stamp have both been given and at the request of the giver thanked for. After that we change to America and those who are very much older and have had really have had an entirely different experience not only with all of it but with very much else. In both cases handkerchiefs and Easter and in the one case as a gift and in the other case as reception and careful conditions. Conditions carefully conditions as carefully as carefully as conditions and as ever.

This is the story of an American. An american formerly known as meant as much as that formerly known everywhere where he had been as having been seen often can not replace it all alone and not any more. The reason given is that when can there be a change, changes and occupation. Occupied too. This makes the meaning of what he meant when he had four or five four or five what.

This is the story of a friendship, two sons two and two sons, a man as two and two sons, and a man and as two and two sons. They had neither of them any reason to come again soon. This made it so prettily as an order. Order it.

No one sees more than it for distribution. No, no women. No.

Begin again fairly well. An American woman means that she is to say have it, have it, four four and why should four and four why should four and four and why should four and four, fear, four and four, fear.

The frenchwoman comes away, comes away, fifteen fifteen has never meant that, sixteen has never meant that seventeen has never meant that, if as presents, if as presents easter and if as presents. Hopes to stay.

How many examples make addition subtraction division and long division. To continue as advised.

Another case of a frenchman. A frenchman has had an arrangement that makes it possible that he should read and what should he read. He should read and write. What should he read and write. He should read and write and recite. What should he read and write and recite.

Another case is the case of that American the American of whom it is said can he say so. This American of whom it is said can he say so says practically that he practically says that he unites windows and windows when windows and windows are in their place and he wishes to stop that is to remain where he is.

The example of the American lady who has a fan is the one selected for admiration in the same way the example of the french lady who has a fan is the one selected as the one to be chosen to be an example of an admirable frenchwoman. The next example that is to be noted is that of the french family who nearly came too late for the festival. Every one asked was the celebration as pleasant as it could be and they were all there.

The American family needed no more, no one needed any

more nothing more was needed really nothing more was needed at all. All of them and so forth and very kindly. Will they kindly say so also.

The next example is easily disposed of in this way there is no difference.

The next example may not be used to be used, the next example may be used to show that an aunt and two nieces say that they may make up their minds to stay the nieces may make up their minds to stay and the aunt may make up her mind to let them stay and they may or they may not be asked to stay. Anyway the decision has cost them nothing and so forth. This is principally from them and by them and in a way for them and perhaps beside them. This is in a way before them.

The other example American example the other examples the American example is this both nieces and their aunt have been separated for some time and quite naturally they do not ask it of each other and if so it is refused. There is always some reason given.

More examples make all of it necessary. The difference between the examples is this, one example shows this and the same example never shows anything else. Another example shows something else and in this way something is proved. Approved by all.

A Finish.

More difference the more difference it makes the less trouble there is in making any reference to it.

The trouble with it is that they may be mistaken. The marriage and it is a marriage may mean more. Having met and having met the man and having met the man there he might say that he had never heard of it and he might say that when he heard of it he said that he had not heard of it before. This makes it all the more this makes all the more and as this makes it all the more as much so. Formerly and formally, formally and formerly does it mean that indeed as they said she had not thought so.

On the other side as another side this is the other side. If the man should assume that he was to be married would his brother write to him as his father would have written to him. And would the wife say that her husband had written to his brother as the father would have written to the brother and would he. The occasion did not arise as the brother remained unmarried married again. Another case is this, the father and the mother had a son. The son was young and when he was old enough he married and as his father and his mother said it might easily be that the marriage would be satisfactory.

The American case is this. The father and the mother had not denied it to any one. No one need wonder. And no wonder was and it was no wonder that they all felt that children had that privilege and did not need to remember how often everything was heard. They heard it said.

To say we will wait, to say we wait, waiting for recognition. Take this case. Not excited about that. Take that case. No excitement in that. In that case there is no excitement in that case. That makes what one can out of everything.

The American has nearly five has nearly five has more nearly five. The American has nearly more nearly all five. The French and almost and almost, almost the french and almost. Two and three and their family for this as this with this to this, to decide all decide and decide. Expect recognition.

The American five times laterally, laterally for five times and not to except and to disturb and not to be all so far and as far as that.

Forty-four and forty, make forty-five which is the same as has expected recognition.

The American has expected recognition.

The difference between there is a difference between, what is the difference and their difference, to add to them to be added to them, to divide from them to be divided from them, to be sent away by them and if sent away by them would they be willing are they willing have they spoken of it and have they acted in a way to make it at all likely that they would be prepared to have it happen. This is partly a beginning.

For any other reason there is more of this for a reason, there is more of this for this reason and for the rest of the time as well.

Thought of it, they thought of it, as they thought it as they thought of it as well.

They thought of it as well and very nearly always for this and on this account. No change was made.

Change it for one change it as perhaps may be necessary. They changed it and they changed it.

Change it in a family early way. This is an example. Three months is an example. This is an example. At the end of three months is an example. This is an example as the three months are more than ended it is an example.

The Americans have heard they have heard the Americans and they have heard, the American has heard as the American has heard this.

A new example of indeed and said so. No one and that.

Has many as many, as many, in case of as many, they went on to say as many has many, as many as they went on to say and so soon as soon and as soon, the one thing necessary is and was that there was a mistake in having it as an impression that one was not going to told so at all.

48

After that there is no reason why after that there is no reason why.

Can it be seen that these two last that these last two differ from one another.

Another difference if and another difference.

After that in the middle of it, after that in the middle of it after that in the middle of it they have to as much as if they told you what they would do just as if they had preferred to, preferred to. Changed to preferred to. Just as if they had to changed to preferred to.

The American can say changed to preferred to the American can say or say the American can say to say, to say can say changed to can say to say changed to to say can say to changed to to preferred to to say to preferred to to changed to to say to say to can say.

Very occupied with that and very occupied with that and here and very occupied with that.

And there and not and there and not and not there.

Here and there and not and very occupied as occupied as that.

And there and there and not as here and there and not and not here and not there, there and not here. There and there and as not here and there.

Here and occupied, occupied and here occupied as that.

There and not there and not and as there and as not there and not, as not there.

And here. For instance as occupied as that. Here and for instance here in this instance here occupied as that.

There occupied as that there. This is a new this is a nuisance, this is news too, this is new too, this is not new too. As occupied as that in this instance.

Here, come here. No one says come here here.

There, come here, they say come here there.

To guess which is which.
Which is which.
Guess.
Two guess.
Which is which.
Guess which is which.
To guess which is which.
Which is which.
The first one here.
The one here.
Guess which is which.
I guess which is which.
The first there.
Which is which.
Here and there.
Which is which.
To guess which is which.
To guess which is which here which is which there. Which is which.
To guess which is which.
If to guess which is which, if to guess which is which, to guess.
Which is which.

5.

Near East or Chicago
A Description

At east, and ingredients, and east and ingredients, and east and ingredients and east and east and and east and ingredients.

And east and ingredients.

Having never been having never been and explaining explaining having been once having been, having been having never been once explaining once having been having been never having been never having been there.

Some one might sell it to somebody. Obviously not.

Clearly counting afterwards at first, clearly counting at first clearly counting afterwards at first.

Remembered to remind, and remembered to remind and at once and later and the same. In this and might, might be ready yet.

Supposing no one asked a question. What would be the answer.

Supposing no one hurried four how many would there be if the difference was known.

Supposing it was a great deal would there be in return would there be mountains in return or would there be mountains in return.

The first time and a memory of it, the first time and a memory of it. Not at all as established and not in there.

Forgetting tables forgetting their tables forgetting the tables.

Forgetting tables.
In forgetting tables.
After all.
No one likes that no one like that no one like that no one
likes that, no one likes that.
And not many of them.
How many in each city, how many in each city in each
city how many who are born in each city are born in a city,
how many are born in a city how many are born in each
city how many are born in each city how many are born
in a city.
It is a remarkable question.
For instance if six, if six for instance for instance if six if
for instance six.
Away from here here and away from here.
For instance if six if six here if six away from here if six
away from here for instance if six here for instance if six
away from here.
The first one and not another, the first one the second, the
second one the second one the first one the second one the
second one the first one the second one. The third one, one
and one and the third one the fourth one the fifth one the
sixth one the one and the added one and the one and the
fifth one and the sixth one.
Knew one, and knew one.
Knew one and knew one and knew one when had not
known one. Knowing one.
It is not exciting knowing one.
It is not exciting.
It is not exciting.
Knowing one is not exciting.
It is not exciting.

Knowing one is not exciting.

Knowing that one.

Knowing the first one it is not exciting knowing the first one. It is not exciting knowing one, it is not exciting knowing the one it is not exciting knowing the first one, it is not exciting knowing the first one it is not exciting knowing one.

It is not exciting it is not exciting knowing one it is not exciting knowing the first one it is not exciting knowing the first one it is not exciting, it is not exciting knowing one.

Not knowing one it is not exciting not knowing one it is not exciting it is not exciting it is not exciting it is not exciting not knowing one.

Having had it in the way having had it anyway having had it anyway having had it in that way, having had it.

The difference between recent and neglect. The difference between neglect and sent and sent and center. The difference between neglect and center, the difference between recent and neglect and neglect and center the difference between recent and neglect and center. The difference between recent and neglect and center.

It was at once at once and it was at once.

If in numbers and numbered a quarter past is not the same, as in division of minutes. A quarter past is not the same as a division of minutes and the minutes. A division into minutes and the minutes.

And had and heard it. In this way mountains are understood.

A considerable time after this there came to be asked of them in arranging would they go and in and ultimately ultimately used to to be used and after this in description and after this and description, to be used to and after this and description. Not important to it at all at all at all, at all and at all.

Having had no occasion to have and to have patiently, having had no occasion at all and having had and not patiently having had patiently having had and having at all, having had no occasion at all and having had patiently and having had and having had patiently and having patiently and having had at all, having had no occasion and at all and having had patiently and having had no occasion at all.

The next time and connecting.

If one and one and as in case of patiently and had patiently and having had and had, as much as it again.

The next time and connecting.

Would men differ from women.

This might be distress.

Would men differ.

This might be distress.

In added and in added and in added and in and in added.

Thirty-three are equal and thirty-three are equal.

Thirty-three are as equal. Equally thirty-three are as equal.

Having forgotten and one.

Had it has had to have it, Fanny has had to have it Fanny has had.

The third one known the fourth one known, the fourth one to be known the fifth one to be known.

The fourth one to be known.

Not having had it not having had to have it, and now, now as likely to attend to it now and then. To be disturbed by having two come back, to be disturbed by having five invited, to be disturbed by having one and one to be disturbed by baskets and not to be disturbed as if at once. At once and later.

To be disturbed by no means to be disturbed, to be disturbed, by no means, to be disturbed, to be disturbed and by no means and by no means to be disturbed.

Did they intend did they intend to did they intend to do did they intend it did they intend to attend to did they intend to attend to it, did they they attend did they attend to it did they intend to attend to it did they intend to attend did they intend to do it did they intend to attend to it.

In seeming and not at present and quickly and two at once and separately and as having begun and to begin and one and one and not first so that it was as much in advance.

Did they find did they find did they find and no one can say did they find and did they find and did they find and did they find their and did they find that explanation. It was as much as it was as much as it was as much as much as pearls as much as. And did they find that as it did not occur and to occur occur often.

If he if he and if he had two sons. If she had two sons and they came home, if she had two sons and they came home. Easily not at once and five altogether.

Does it make it certain that they asked for wishes. Wishes may be desires or a wish.

When he said and he said it at once, when he said we are now and he said it at once.

Not to remind him.

When he said and just as long and he said and just as long as he said it.

And to remind him.

As he said and he said that he went further.

How did he feel about inches.

He felt he always felt he always had felt more than as much.

How did he feel about it. He felt about it.

Interested in it at all.

The next time that there was an instance of it he was not confused because he knew that one hand holds the other.

For them and for them and for them he had this intention.

To recapitulate.

Older.

Older.

And older.

Younger.

And younger.

Older and younger.

And older and younger.

To recapitulate.

He had this use for them.

And for him.

He had this use for him.

To recapitulate.

He had this use for him.

He had this use for them.

At once and not reminded.

Twice and not reminded.

Not reminded, twice and not reminded.

Twice and not reminded.

Once and not reminded.

Once and not reminded.

Twice and not reminded.

He had this use for him.

He had this use for them.

He had this use for them.

He had this use for him.

Once and not reminded.

He had this use for him.

Not reminded.

It is as interesting as in the case of that and this and not at all and at once and for this and because and how it happened and increased.

Having decided absolutely.

This has been done again.

As much.

As famous and as for it.

As famous for it.

He knew that.

When he went and what.

He knew how.

When he had it now.

He knew where.

And at once and care.

He knew which.

When he had it and at once and two.

This made three at once.

This made three at once at once.

Five and two denied.

Three and six beside.

One and two at once.

And forty.

Coming to count counting is clever.

Accountable.

This makes it easy to remind to remind him of it. It is not often done it may be said not to be done not to be done never to be done.

Beginning with fifty and fifty makes fifty-five.

As early as that.

Finally the first time that there was an occasion to know about it was the time when it was past and as past and presently as past and not remembered not only remembered and furthermore burning and furthermore remembered and furthermore. After this and not in there and not of it and not because of it and nearly in the middle that is further away.

After that not at once and certainly not more and more. This and all and care and see.

At once and later and at once and later and beyond and not at all beside and furthermore. It could easily be seen additionally and not at all.

Not at all and to answer.

The next time and so much after having hid or hid.

Having had or having hid or having hidden had or hid it.

There was so much and as much and after noon. In there and either.

He denies it.

All come all come all come and all come, all come all come all come and all come come and as much and as it were refusing to confide the doubt to Professor McClintock.

Very good before, very good before and after and very good before and very good before and after.

If it was easy to be old if it was easy easier, if it was easy to be old if it was easy to be old if it was easy to be old if it was easy if it was easy to be old if it was easy to be old.

The next time that all of them are as actively as that, the next time that all of them are as actively as all that the next time that all of them are as actively as all that all of them as actively, all of them as actively as all that all of them the next time that all of them are as actively as that.

They are as whether as a first and last four as not used for horses as not bound to be needed to be needed to to and care, as not bound to be needed, to and care and bound to be needed and not to and care and bound to be needed to and care and bound to be needed.

If to have and to turn over the edge and to have returned a mother to a father makes it makes it as a mixture of later. Not late at all. To them both.

FINIS.

6.

Among Negroes

A story of the Three of you Josephine Baker Maud de Forrest and Ida Lewelyn and Mr. and Mrs. Paul Robeson and as they never met and as they never met. Naturally. They were made to be alike they were not made to be alike. Naturally. Josephine Baker Maud de Forrest and Ida Lewelyn. Naturally. Mr. and Mrs. Paul Robeson. Naturally. After all who made habit have it.

When she and they have sat and they are as they are sitting who means whom. As easily as ever.

Josephine Baker has to have where she is to have been from. Maud de Forrest has to have her mother as her father and her pretty nearly as nicely. Ida Lewelyn has to be very likely has to be used to having sisters. All three of them are alike. They resemble also resemble their mother. This makes them speak casually. What did they do. They met too. Mr. and Mrs. Paul Robeson have not been present they have never been present. After a while they could never have been present and now in a little time and now. Begin now.

The life of trees and the length of life of trees. As the length of life as the length of life of trees.

Returning to following.

Maud de Forrest was often in Washington Washington and Washington. Maud de Forrest having often been in Washington was born in Washington Maud de Forrest was born in Washington. She knew she knew she did not believe that she would have gone further than a long distance a long distance from there. She answered and she knew what she was asking when she said if you go there that way that way and very well after all very never very and very very very told very. Very whom. They meet to miss and mistaken. A long able to not to not and long and having it as easily. It is very easy altogether and naturally and who would who would have pearls and have girls. Not she.

She Maud de Forrest wanted very much to come and so it was arranged that she would be able to.

Consider it as coming and came.

When Maud de Forrest and Ida Lewelyn and Josephine Baker and Miss Dudley Miss Dudley preferred her and Josephine Baker and Ida Lewelyn and not Ida Lewelyn and Maud de Forrest and not Maud de Forrest and Josephine Baker and not Josephine Baker and Miss Dudley preferred it.

Miss Dudley preferred it.

Josephine Baker Josephine Baker and Miss Dudley preferred it.

The next time that there are and that they are reading not reading made easy and not large or largest not largest trees and not they did not need it either or three.

Josephine Baker was accustomed to it.

She looked at me as if I knew her when she did like not that but a little while and does not sound might it does sound so. This is a tenner tenner too. Intend to. Maud de Forrest met to go and to go. Josephine Baker and it was not because she had not and Ida Lewelyn because they meant to part because they had all wished it as alike as if they had more than when they had had had had and had had it. Had it makes a noon.

Two fifty two two fifty three. And not introduced. Not introduced asked to sing again. Asked to sing again and who is they may. She says it was Josephine Baker. He says it is Maud de Forrest. They did not say. She said it was Maud de Forrest. She said it was Josephine Baker. They leave out she said it was Josephine Baker. They leave out he said it was Maud de Forrest. They leave out she she said it was Josephine Baker. They leave out she said it was Maud de Forrest. She said it was Josephine Baker.

A little use in use used is a use a little use in use used is a use use is a little use in use. Used is a little use in used used is a use a little use in use.

Let it be that they think we we have a week we have a week week and week let it be.

Let it be that to have meant had they and not entirely twenty-five twenty-five is in a difference beween Wednesday and Friday.

Mr. and Mrs. Robeson came Friday they had ready they had had ready and as between in there in here and there and there they had in that older older is as old is Friday older than Wednesday is Wednesday older is Friday older not as younger and older not as older and not as younger in their best. The difference between as best.

She need never regret that she had it around it around it she had it. She need never regret that she had it around it she need never regret that around it that she had it around it.

In a little Monday and Tuesday and Wednesday and Thursday and Friday.

Always longer.

7.

Business in Baltimore

Nor narrow, long.
Julian is two.
How many and well.
And days and sank.
Thanks to having.
Business in Baltimore thanks to having and days and sank
how many and well Julian is two not narrow, long.
Julian is two how many and well thanks to having.
Once upon a time Baltimore was necessary.
How and would it be dressed if they had divided a bank
and tan. It connected at once it connected twice it con-
nected doors and floors.
This is in May.
So they say.
How many places for scales are there in it.
Weigh once a day.
In Baltimore there are the ferns the miles the pears the
cellars and the coins.
After that the large and small stones or stepping stones.
This is why they have every reason to be arranged and every
morning to be morning and every evening to be evening.
This is the reason why they have every Sunday and Tuesday
and Monday.
Who finds minds and who lines shines and two kinds finds
and two kinds minds. Minds it. She never wanted to leave
Baltimore anywhere and was it.

Business in Baltimore.

He did and peppers see he did and three.

He did and three he did and see he did and three and see and he did and peppers see and peppers see and three he did.

It is so easy to have felt needed and shielded and succeeded and decided and widened and waited. No waiting for him Saturday Monday and Thursday.

All of them are devoted to it to doing what was done when it was begun and afterwards all sashes are old. Forget wills. The best and finally the first, the first and formerly the rest all of it as they have it to do to do to do already in their house. Suppose in walking up and down they sat around. Imagine vines, vines are not had here imagine vines that are not to be had here and imagine rubbers had here and imagine working working in blue that means over it. Each one of these had to give away had to have to had to give way. How many others brothers and fathers.

He had held him he had held her he had held it for him he had held it for her, he had hold of it, and he had had days. How many days pay, how much of a day pays and how difficultly from thinking. I think I thought I said I sought I fell I fought I had I ought to have meant to be mine.

Not as funny as yet.

Imagining up and down. How many generations make five.

If another marries her brother, if another marries their brother, if their brother marries another, if their brother and a brother marry another and the sister how many pairs are there of it.

It is easy not to be older than that.

Do you hear me.

It is easier.

How many papers can make more papers and how many

64

have to have her. Have to have her. How many papers can make more papers and how many have to have to have it. How many have to have to have it and how many papers make more papers. It makes a little door to-day.

Put it there for him to see. He knew how and how to have he knew how to have and accepted so much as much or much much of it for it, for it is and in either direction might be saved, saved or so and while it is while it is while it is near near while it is while it is near having monthly in use. To hear them and as it has to be at and for and as it has to be for and mine and as it has to be powder and ice and as it has to be and as it has to be louder and there and as it has to be louder and there and I hear it.

And in there.

When he could not remember that when he could not remember it at all when he could remember it all and when he could remember it all. It started and parted, partly to them and for most. Foremost is a way they have to have used here.

The first time they ever had it, heard it and had it, the first time they ever had it.

In their favor as a favor as a favor or favorable.

Having forgotten how it sounds, have they forgotten all the sound remind them.

The first reason for having seven is six and a half, six and a half and as seldom. After that the real reason for six more than a half and as seldom the real reason for six more and a half and as seldom is six more six more and a half more and six more and a half more and six more and a half more and seldom.

Please put it in paper there.

A little place and for fortunately. Did he and they have a lake to-day. Nearly.

Having at it and at once a noise and it, it could be just as much more also. Have a sound of or a sound of or, or Alice. Miss Alice is might it.

The very easy how do red horses have a pair. This makes Arthur and no name. He made him go.

Come near come nearly come nearly come near come near come nearly. Come near. Come near come nearly. He had a haul and I said do you do that and he did and he said not to-day. Anybody can say not to-day.

There was once upon a time a selfish boy and a selfish man, there was once upon a time a selfish man. There was once upon a time a selfish man. There was once upon a time there was once upon a time a selfish man there was once upon a time a selfish boy there was once upon a time a selfish boy there was once upon a time a selfish boy there was once upon a time a selfish man. How selfish. There was once upon a time a selfish man. There was once upon a time a selfish boy, how once upon a time a selfish boy how once upon a time a selfish man.

Nobody knows whose wedding shows it to them. Business in Baltimore makes a wedding first at first business in Baltimore makes a wedding at first first. Business in Baltimore makes a wedding at first at first. Business in Baltimore makes a wedding at first at first first. Business in Baltimore makes a wedding first at first. Business in Baltimore at first makes a wedding first makes a wedding at first. Business in Baltimore makes a wedding at first.

Business in Baltimore makes a wedding at first.

Business in Baltimore at first.

In heights and whites, in whites and lights, in lights in sizes, in sizes in sides and in wise, or as wise or wiser. This not to be the first to know.

To know.

Altogether older, older altogether.

Not following hearing or a son or another. No one spells mother or brother.

To them or then or then by then it was mostly done by them.

Who has had had it had. Had it, he had it and following he had it, he had it. Following he had it.

Business in Baltimore following he had it. Business in Baltimore following he had it following he had had it. Business in Baltimore following he had had it. Following he had had it following he had had it business in Baltimore following he had had it.

Business in Baltimore.

How easy it is to see voices. How easy it is to see.

How easy it is to see voices and very much of it put as a rug. Supposing a whole floor was covered and on the cover where he stands has a place for it which is attached to them and of this kind. Could it have been made before a boat and no one follows. How many have had hands.

When they were sung to sung to see when they were sung to sung among when they were snugly sung to see, see seeds for that to eat and for and have the size and no more satchels made at all. Satchels may be held loosely. When they are sung and sung and sung and little have to have a hand and hand and two and two hands too, and too and two and handled too to them, handed to them, hand and hands. Hands high. This can be Baltimore and or and Baltimore and for and Baltimore and more and Baltimore and for and Baltimore and or. It does not sound like it.

When he older than that when he older than this when he older than this when he as old as he is, he is as old as he is, he is as old he is as old and would they know that fifty are fairly plenty of later hats. Hats cannot be used as mats not for selling or for much as much. He certainly was amused by it.

Devoted to having a whole a half a half a whole, a whole or told it. Devoted to having a half, a whole a whole or told or it. Devoted to having a whole a half a half a whole a whole or told it. Devoted to having a half a whole a whole a whole a half a whole or told it.

She did see fortunes fade.

Who did see fortunes fade.

Nobody saw fortunes fade. Nobody saw fortunes nobody saw fortunes fade.

A whole a half a half a whole, fortunes fade who never saw fortunes fade he never saw fortunes fade. A half a whole he never saw he never saw fortunes he never saw fortunes fade or faded. He never saw fortunes he never saw fortunes fade.

How much business is there in Baltimore.

And how many are there in business in Baltimore.

And how have they had to have business in Baltimore.

And how has it been how has it been how has he been in business in Baltimore.

He has been in business in Baltimore and before and before he was in business in Baltimore he was not in business he was not in business before he was in business in Baltimore.

He had been in business before he had been in business in Baltimore he had been in business before in Baltimore. How had he been in business in Baltimore. He had been in business before in Baltimore he had not been in business before he was in business in Baltimore.

Business in Baltimore before, before business, before business in Baltimore.

Business in Baltimore is business in Baltimore.
Business in Baltimore in business in Baltimore and business in Baltimore is this business in Baltimore.
How many more are there in business in Baltimore than there were before.
How many more are in business in Baltimore than were in business in Baltimore before.
This business in Baltimore.
That business in Baltimore.
A business in Baltimore.
Business in Baltimore.
Who says business in Baltimore. Who says business in Baltimore and before, and who says business in Baltimore more business in Baltimore more business in Baltimore than before.
Pleases me, and while they have to have eaten eaten it, and eaten eaten it and eaten eaten it eaten eaten eaten eaten eaten it. Then a list is useful. Useful soon, useful as soon. As useful as soon. As useful as soon. Some time and shown. Who has to say so say so. They easily have after and soon.
It was said at once to them that they had it. Afterwards it was said at once to them that they had it. Afterwards it was at once said to them that they had it. It was said to them it was afterwards said to them at once that they had it. It was afterwards said at once said to them afterwards said to them that they had it. It was afterwards said to them that they had it. It was afterwards at once said to them that they had it.
How much easier how much easier, how much easier and how much easier. Forty makes forty and forty-four makes forty-four and forty-four makes four and forty four makes forty-four. Business in Baltimore makes counting easy.

If he had had and had had given and had had given to him what he had had how many more are there to have held it in this way away. One and he was famous not for that nor for provision nor for in addition nothing, nothing too much, not anything more and it was not said to be said. It takes many times more to make many times more and not to make many times more and not to make many times more many times more. Not many times more. Read riches. Anything that begins with r makes read riches and this is as twice and once and once. Once is it once, twice is it twice is it twice once and is it once twice. This is the way they make the day they make the day they make the day this is the way they make the day, once a day and it is a reason for having heard of it. Now at last it is well known that not because he did he did not hurry he did not hurry because he did and did not hurry and who asked him. That is what they say who asked him.

Forgetting a name.

Not to be transferred to Baltimore and so to say so so much. If you do not hear him speak at all louder then not to speak at all louder, not to speak at all louder not to hear him speak at all louder not to hear him speak at all louder and so not to speak at all louder. He does not speak louder and so not to speak louder and so not to speak louder at all.

She was as well as he was as well as he was as well as she was as well as all that.

All that as well as all that and having forgotten all the same having forgotten having forgotten and all the same all the same as having forgotten and to hear it hear it heard it heard it hear heard it heard it, heard it and all the same as forgotten having heard it all the same and all the same and having forgotten and having heard and all the same. Having heard it all the same having heard hear it hear it all the same having forgotten and hear it and having forgotten and hear it and all the same and all the same and hear it and heard it.

So much and so much farther as much and as much farther, and as much farther and so much and hear it and having heard it and all the same and having heard it and all the same and hear it and all the same and hear it and heard and having heard and all the same and hear it. Here and hear it. They are all the same as heard it as hear it all the same as heard it all the same and as heard it. All the same and heard and as heard it and as heard it and as all the same and heard it. All the same. Hear it. All the same hear it all the same.

The same examples are the same and just the same and always the same and the same examples are just the same and are the same and always the same. The same examples are just the same and they are very sorry for it. So is not business in Baltimore. And so it is not and so is it not and as it is not and as it is and as it is not the same more than the same. This sounds as if they said it and it sounds as if they meant it and it sounds as if they meant it and it sounds as if they meant and as if they meant it. Everybody is disappointed in Julian's cousin Julian's cousin too, everybody is also disappointed is disappointed in Julian's cousin too. Julian and everybody is disappointed in Julian's cousin and everybody too is disappointed in Julian's cousin too. How many days are there for it. There are as many days for it as there are ways to see how they do it. Do it too. Julian and a cousin too. Two and two, and two and two and lists and remembered and lists. To commence back further and just as far and as far back and just as far back. Just as far back as that. Just as far back as that and Julian remembers just as far back as that and Julian remembers just as far back and remembers Julian remembers just as far back as that.

Everybody knows that anybody shows shows it as soon as soon and at noon as carefully noon as carefully soon, everybody knows, everybody shows, everybody shows anybody knows carefully as soon carefully and noon carefully at noon everybody knows everybody shows carefully at noon carefully soon carefully soon carefully at noon, everybody knows carefully at noon carefully as soon anybody knows everybody shows everybody shows everybody knows carefully as soon, anybody knows carefully as soon, anybody knows carefully at noon everybody knows carefully as soon everybody knows carefully as soon, anybody knows carefully as soon everybody knows carefully as soon.

Everybody knows carefully as soon, everybody knows carefully at noon everybody knows carefully as soon.

Entirely exposed too.

And how many in passing turn around. Just how many in passing just how many turn around. One can always tell the difference between snowy and cloudy everybody can always tell some difference between cloudy and snowy. Every one can always tell some difference.

Every one can always tell some difference between cloudy and cloudy between snowy and snowy between cloudy and snowy between snowy and cloudy.

Not as to dinner and dinner.

How many are a hundred and how many are two hundred and how many are a million and three. This is for them to answer and in this way more in Baltimore. Business in Baltimore consists of how many and how often and more at once and a half of them there.

Business in Baltimore is always a share a share and care to

care and where where in Baltimore. Where in Baltimore. How many kinds are there in it.

There are many and as many there are as many as there are streets, corners, places, rivers and trees in Baltimore. Squares can be mentioned too and stones and little and at once to approach. Who changes all changes.

All changes who changes.

Do not hurry to winter and to summer. Do not hurry to winter. Do not hurry to summer. Do not hurry to summer. Not to hurry to winter. Not to hurry to winter and to summer and to winter and not to hurry to summer and not to hurry to winter.

He can hear they can hear they can hear that they do hear her. They can hear that they do hear him. They can hear that they do hear him. They can hear that they do hear her. They can hear that they can hear him.

They can hear winter, they can hear summer they can hear that they do hear summer, they can hear that they do hear that they can hear winter, they can hear summer they can hear winter. They can hear that they hear him they can hear that they can hear her they do hear that they can hear that they do hear her that they do hear winter that they do hear her that they can hear her that they can hear that they do hear him that they do hear him that they can hear that they do hear that they hear that they can hear summer and hear hear her here hear him here that they can hear her that they can hear. They do hear that they can hear winter. They do hear that they can hear summer.

Business in Baltimore for them and with them with them and as a tree is bought. How is a tree bought. Business in Baltimore and for them and by them and is bought how is it to be bought and where is it to be bought. Business in Baltimore and for them and adding it to them and as it has

73

the half of the whole and the whole is more if it is best shown to be more used than it was here and nearly. This and a result. Take it in place, take it to a place take it for a place and places and to place and placed. Placed and placing should a daughter be a mother. Placed and placing should a father be a brother. Placed and placing should a mother be a sister altogether. All this makes it easy that very many say so and very many do so and very many do so and very many say so.

He can so easily amuse himself and so can he so very easily amuse himself and so can he so very easily and so can he so very easily amuse himself and so can he so very easily and so can he so very easily amuse himself and as it were to be they had to have it largely and more and when they needed it all. To begin.

How many houses were there in it. And to go on. And how many houses were there in it.

How to depend upon it. And how many houses were there in it. And how to depend upon it and how many houses were there in it. How many houses are there in it.

There were as many houses as there were in it.

There were as many houses in it as there were as many houses in it. There are as many houses in it. How many houses are there in it. There are as many houses as there are in it. After that streets, corners, connections and ways of walking. There were more houses than there were in it. There were more corners than there were in it. There were more streets than there were in it. How many streets are there in it. How many corners are there in it. How many streets are there in it. How many houses were there in it. Everybody counting. Call somebody Hortense. Please do. And David. Please do.

A little makes it all stop and stopped. A little makes it all stopped and stop. A little makes it all stop. A little makes it all stopped.

It is a great pleasure for Hilda and for William for William and for Hilda. It is a great pleasure for either. If a home and a house and as often as hurry and hurried, they need to and do, they need to do they did need to they did and they did need to and they do and they do and they did need to do it too. Does she look as much like it as the newspaper would suggest.

Plainly make it mine. Plainly make it plainly make it mine. This is as least not as well said as ever.

Having forgotten to hear, what and having forgotten to hear what had not been forgotten and not forgotten to hear.

They have please they have please they have please. Business in Baltimore they have please.

Did they like five.

Did they like five of five.

Business in Baltimore and more. More seated.

Business in Baltimore need never be finished here when it is there when it is commenced there when it is completed here when it is added to here when it is established there. In this they mean he means to too and two.

Never to be used at last to last and never as it was as if it was a horse. They have no use for horses.

Never as it was as if it was because they had to have a way of counting one to make one.

Could be sitting around faced that way and lean and if he did would he not having been as payed follow to a home. Follow to a home for him.

Two cannot make room for two and two both seated cannot make room for two both seated. Two both seated cannot make room for two both seated.

75

This is one date.

Two cannot make room for two both seated.

Yes and yes and more and yes and why and yes and yes and why and yes. A new better and best and yes and yes and better and most and yes and yes and better and best and yes and yes and more and best and better and most and yes and yes. And yes and yes and better and yes and more and yes and better and yes, and yes and yes and more and yes and better and yes and more and yes and yes and yes and more and best and yes and yes and better and most and yes and yes and more and better and best and most and yes and yes and most and better and yes and yes and most and more and yes and yes, and more and yes and yes and better and yes and yes and most and yes and yes and best and yes and yes and better and yes and more and yes and best and yes and better and yes and more and yes and most and yes and more and yes and yes and better and yes and yes and most and yes and yes and best and yes and yes and yes and yes and better and most and yes and yes and better and most and yes and yes and more and most and yes and yes and better and most and yes and yes and more and better and yes and yes and yes and yes and more and best and yes and yes and more and best and yes and yes and more and yes and yes and best and yes and yes and more and yes and yes and better and yes and yes and best and yes and yes and more and yes and yes and better and yes and yes. And yes and yes and and more and better and yes and yes and better and yes and yes and more and yes and yes and better and and yes and yes and better and yes and yes and more and yes and yes and best and better and yes and yes and most and more and yes and yes and yes and yes and better and yes and best and most and better and more and best and better and yes and yes and yes and yes and yes and yes and more and yes and yes and better and yes and yes and more and yes and yes. And more and yes and yes. And more and better and yes and yes and best and more and yes and yes and better and yes and yes and most and yes and yes and best and more and yes and yes and yes and yes and better and more and better and yes and yes and most and better and more and yes and yes and yes and yes. And better and yes and yes and more and yes and yes and yes and yes and more and best and better and most and best and better and most and more and more and most and better and yes and yes.

8.

Scenes from the Door

THE FORD

It is earnest.
Aunt Pauline is earnest.
We are earnest.
We are united.
Then we see.

RED FACES

Red flags the reason for pretty flags.
And ribbons.
Ribbons of flags,
And wearing material
Reason for wearing material.
Give pleasure.
Can you give me the regions.
The regions and the land.
The regions and wheels.
All wheels are perfect.
Enthusiasm.

WHAT IS THIS

You can't say it's war.
I love conversation.
Do you like it printed.
I like it descriptive.

Not very descriptive.
Not very descriptive.
I like it to come easily
Naturally
And then.
Crystal and cross.
Does not lie on moss.
The three ships.
You mean washing the ships.
One was a lady.
A nun.
She begged meat
Two were husband and wife.
They had a rich father-in-law to the husband.
He did dry cleaning.
And the third one.
A woman.
She washed.
Clothes.
Then this is the way we were helped.
Not interested
We are very much interested.

DAUGHTER

Why is the world at peace.
This may astonish you a little but when you realise how
easily Mrs. Charles Bianco sells the work of American
painters to American millionaires you will recognise that
authorities are constrained to be relieved. Let me tell you a
story. A painter loved a woman. A musician did not sing.
A South African loved books. An American was a woman
and needed help. Are Americans the same as incubators.
But this is the rest of the story. He became an authority.

A RADICAL EXPERT

Can you please by asking what is expert. And then we met
one another. I do not think it right. Marksman. Expert.
Loaf. Potatoe bread. Sugar Card. Leaf. And mortar. What
is the meaning of white wash. The upper wall.
That sounds well.
And then we sinned.
A great many jews say so.

AMERICA

Once in English they said America. Was it English to them.
Once they said Belgian.
We like a fog.
Do you for weather.
Are we brave.
Are we true.
Have we the national colour.
Can we stand ditches.
Can we mean well.
Do we talk together.
Have we red cross.
A great many people speak of feet.
And socks.

9.

A Patriotic Leading

Verse I
Indeed indeed.
Can you see.
The stars.
And regularly the precious treasure.
What do we love without measure.
We know.

Verse II
We suspect the second man.

Verse III
We are worthy of everything that happens.
You mean weddings.
Naturally I mean weddings.

Verse IV
And then we are.
Hail to the nation.

Verse V
Do you think we believe it.

Verse VI
It is that or bust.

Verse VII
We cannot bust.

Verse VIII
Thank you.

Verse IX
Thank you so much.

10.

Are There Six or Another Question

One — Are there six.
Two — Or another question.
One — Are there six.
Two — Or another question.
Two — Are there six.
One — Or another question.
Two — Are there six
Two — Or another question.

11.

Three Leagues

A LEAGUE

Why don't you visit your brother with a girl he doesn't know.
And in the midst of emigration we have wishes to bestow.
We gather that the West is wet and fully ready to flow.
We gather that the East is wet and very ready to say so.
We gather that we wonder and we gather that it is in respect to all of us that we think.
Let us stray.
Do you want a baby. A round one or a pink one.

MORE LEAGUE

A vote all around
A coat all around
A leather pin and a dusty hat
We refuse, I refuse.
Some surprise a word. Some surprise a third.
Is there a mother
Is there a cousin.

EVENTS

The President and the President
And he says he is not dead.

And indeed in dying do we encourage prejudices.
He bows his head and then he is dead.
We meet reluctantly with opposition.
We hope that every one will be satisfied with themselves.
We believe in further wishes.

12.

Allen Tanner

At in all as in as with as in as with as when Allen.

Never to be three as we as three tree, it is coming to be like it. Allen it is coming to be like it. Allen it is all as is as when as then Allen it is coming to be like it three as in like it.

Never is never is never as never as never to this to be could it be three.

George Henry and Louis.

Allen Allen when Allen Allen in and when Allen Allen when in and when Allen Allen in Allen in Ellen in Allen in and in Ellen and Allen in and in end in in an end Ellen an in in an end Allen.

Deed and double deed led and dairy led lay and lain and gait and go here and gain and gone and give and geography and join and gesture and able and gave and able and dear and able and known and do and down and little and Paul and does and disperse and days and so so which is mine so which is black so which so which black which so which so so which so so so which so so which so which so which is black.

Allen make a place in post post post it in make a place in post it in make a place in post it in Allen make a place in post it in Allen in post it in Allen in post it in Allen it in Allen make a post in post it in Allen post it in.

Make a place in post it in.

Allen who win in win an win Allen. Who win who win in win who can win in win who can win in win who can win

who can win in can win who in can win can win in win who
in can win in can win can win in win in who can win in can
win in Allen. Ask to have it eat it meet it ask to have it meet
it eat it ask to have it meet it meet it eat eat it asked to have
it eat it meet it ask to have it ask to have it eat it meet it ask
to have it let it be their shone shone with them. Shone with
them like if with shone with them.
In with in very left to be near them.
In in inches feet and left all may may may may may come
may may may may. In in left in may in all in may come
may.
He had a horse named Nelly Nelly is your name. He had a
house named Ella and Allen Ellen is your name. He had a
hand named Bannie Bannie is your name. He had a like it
like like it like it to make it make make it be why is red
white why light it if it is not night and day. Not night and
day. Changed to Allen. Not night and day. Changed to
changed too. Not night and day changed too not night
and day not night and day changed to not night and day
changed to not night and day not night and day not
changed to not not changed to night and day not changed
to not not not night and day not changed to not changed
to not changed to not changed to not night and day. Not
changed to Allen not night and day. Not changed to not
changed to night and day.
It can be so night to see. See he saw. Night and day not to
change to not to not to not to not to night to night to not to
night to night to not to night to not to. Not to change to
not to night to not to. They this the than time to may
to-day.
Not to change to night to day to not to-day to day. Not to
change to night to day.

13.

Emily Chadbourne

Can you listen to Ellen.
Any one can eat a round melon.
Can you settle a taste.
Not in haste not in haste not in haste slowly, not in pearls.
Braids are straight and we ate sacks and sacks of corn.
Look and listen to the sea, see what we can never see, sea for
me, see for me look and illustrate the sea.
The sea comes from Boston to China and Japan. It comes
from inland and from the top. It causes catarrh.
Not a saleable surface, a surface that is rigid is ruined and
a surface that is certain is cloudy and a surface that is missed
is widowed and a surface that is mild is raised and a surface
that has nights is harmless and a surface that meadows is
gracious and a surface that is loosed is smiling and a surface
that is mine is mine. And where do you mind what you hear.
Leaves of distress leave distress a mess, leave a mess for mess
distress. Can not you think and swim.
I cannot make the sound of her voice I cant make the sound
of her voice I cannot make the sound of her voice. Arise
and sit and message.
What does a message say. A message does not say I pray, I
pray that you may have come to-day. A message does not
say, what does she say.
Cards of coloured elections.
I wish it were grey. And can you sneeze readily. I can so
easily wish to disturb, I can so easily wish to be disturbed,

I can so easily wish to reserve and reward. I do not use a word.

Can you smile.

Can you pile the wood awhile.

Can you smile and pile the veils awhile.

Were you expectant, were they expectant were they expecting women.

And what is nervousness. We understand speeches and religion and underpinning and leaves and even Chinamen. We understand so much.

She, she cannot be me, she is the center of the sleeve, I am never surprised by an arm.

Can you use a minute.

Really what can you mean by waste. Waste away.

No friend of mine says that.

And then we smiled at Emily.

14.

Idem the Same

A VALENTINE TO SHERWOOD ANDERSON

I knew too that through them I knew too that he was through, I knew too that he threw them, I knew too that they were through, I knew too I knew too, I knew I knew them.

I knew to them.

If they tear a hunter through, if they tear through a hunter, if they tear through a hunt and a hunter, if they tear through the different sizes of the six, the different sizes of the six which are these, a woman with a white package under one arm and a black package under the other arm and dressed in brown with a white blouse, the second Saint Joseph the third a hunter in a blue coat and black garters and a plaid cap, a fourth a knife grinder who is full faced and a very little woman with black hair and a yellow hat and an excellently smiling appropriate soldier. All these as you please.

In the meantime example of the same lily. In this way please have you rung.

WHAT DO I SEE

A very little snail.
A medium sized turkey.
A small band of sheep.
A fair orange tree.

All nice wives are like that.
Listen to them from here.
Oh.
You did not have an answer.
Here.
Yes.

A VERY VALENTINE

Very fine is my valentine.
Very fine and very mine.
Very mine is my valentine very mine and very fine.
Very fine is my valentine and mine, very fine very mine and
mine is my valentine.

WHY DO YOU FEEL DIFFERENTLY

Why do you feel differently about a very little snail and a
big one.
Why do you feel differently about a medium sized turkey
and a very large one.
Why do you feel differently about a small band of sheep
and several sheep that are riding.
Why do you feel differently about a fair orange tree and one
that has blossoms as well.
Oh very well.
All nice wives are like that.

To Be
No Please
To Be
They can please
Not to be
Do they please.
Not to be

Do they not please
Yes please.
Do they please
No please.
Do they not please
No please.
Do they please.
Please.
If you please.
And if you please
And if they please
And they please.
To be pleased
Not to be pleased.
Not to be displeased.
To be pleased and to please.

KNEELING

One two three four five six seven eight nine and ten.
The tenth is a little one kneeling and giving away a rooster
with this feeling.
I have mentioned one, four five seven eight and nine.
Two is also giving away an animal.
Three is changed as to disposition.
Six is in question if we mean mother and daughter, black
and black caught her, and she offers to be three she offers
it to me.
That is very right and should come out below and just so.

BUNDLES FOR THEM

A History Of Giving Bundles.
We were able to notice that each one in a way carried a

bundle, they were not a trouble to them nor were they all bundles as some of them were chickens some of them pheasants some of them sheep and some of them bundles, they were not a trouble to them and then indeed we learned that it was the principal recreation and they were so arranged that they were not given away, and to-day they were given away.

I will not look at them again.

They will not look for them again.

They have not seen them here again.

They are in there and we hear them again.

In which way are stars brighter than they are. When we have come to this decision. We mention many thousands of buds. And when I close my eyes I see them.

If you hear her snore
It is not before you love her
You love her so that to be her beau is very lovely
She is sweetly there and her curly hair is very lovely
She is sweetly here and I am very near and that is very lovely.
She is my tender sweet and her little feet are stretching out well which is a treat and very lovely
Her little tender nose is between her little eyes which close and are very lovely.
She is very lovely and mine which is very lovely.

ON HER WAY

If you can see why she feels that she kneels if you can see why he knows that he shows what he bestows, if you can see why they share what they share, need we question that there is no doubt that by this time if they had intended to come they would have sent some notice of such intention. She and they and indeed the decision itself is not early dissatisfaction.

15.

Van or Twenty Years After. A Second Portrait of Carl Van Vechten

Twenty years after, as much as twenty years after in as much as twenty years after, after twenty years and so on. It is it is it is it is.
If it and as if it, if it or as if it, if it is as if it, and it is as if it and as if it. Or as if it. More as if it. As more. As more as if it. And if it. And for and as if it.
If it was to be a prize a surprise if it was to be a surprise to realise, if it was to be if it were to be, was it to be. What was it to be. It was to be what it was. And it was. So it was. As it was. As it is. Is it as it as. It is and as it is and as it is. And so and so as it was.
Keep it in sight alright.
Not to the future but to the fuschia.
Tied and untied and that is all there is about it. And as tied and as beside, and as beside and tied. Tied and untied and beside and as beside and as untied and as tied and as untied and as beside. As beside as by and as beside. As by as by the day. By their day and and as it may, may be they will may be they may. Has it been reestablished as not to weigh. Weigh how. How to weigh. Or weigh. Weight, state await, state, late state rate state, state await weight state, in state rate at any rate state weight state as stated. In this way as stated. Only as if when the six sat at the table they all looked for those places together. And each one in that di-

rection so as to speak look down and see the same as weight. As weight for weight as state to state as wait to wait as not so.

Beside.

For arm absolutely for arm.

They reinstate the act of birth.

Bewildering is a nice word but it is not suitable at present.

They meant to be left as they meant to be left, as they meant to be left left and their center, as they meant to be left and and their center. So that in their and do, so that in their and to do. So suddenly and at his request. Get up and give it to him and so suddenly and as his request. Request to request in request, as request, for a request by request, requested, as requested as they requested, or so have it to be nearly there. Why are the three waiting, there are more than three. One two three four five six seven.

As seven.

Seating, regard it as the rapidly increased February.

Seating regard it as the very regard it as their very nearly regard as their very nearly or as the very regard it as the very settled, seating regard it as the very as their very regard it as their very nearly regard it as the very nice, seating regard as their very nearly regard it as the very nice, known and seated seating regard it, seating and regard it, regard it as the very nearly center left and in the center, regard it as the very left and in the center. And so I say so. So and so. That. For. For that. And for that. So and so and for that. And for that and so and so. And so I say so.

Now to fairly see it have, now to fairly see it have and now to fairly see it have. Have and to have. Now to fairly see it have and to have. Naturally.

As naturally, naturally as, as naturally as. As naturally.

Now to fairly see it have as naturally.

16.

Emmet Addis the Doughboy; A Pastoral

If the feeling is so fair and far he fairly feels it, he feels and fairly in his address, addressing them Mr. Byciclist, who goes there who goes with who goes there with you, how do you go there, how do you do, how do you ask how do you ask and how do you ask and how do you go there, and who goes there too. Horses and oxen too and nothing happens to you, Mr. Byciclist you come too.
Emmet Addis the Doughboy questions and questions a few, a few of them any of them answer a few of them all of them answer any one who asks them and questions are asked of them sometimes too. Mr. Byciclist how do you do and where do you go from here and who asks you to come too. As a pastoral too Emmet Addis the Doughboy and who asks him and who asks him and who has asked him.
Second part of Emmet Addis the Doughboy a Pastoral.
The second part of Emmet Addis the doughboy a pastoral deals with his pleasures and his evident replies to questions. Emmet Addis the Doughboy a Pastoral Part two.
In that way, one two, say there stay there stay there one two, in that way one two, say there one two, say there stay there one two, in that way one two. Evidently in this meaning evidences for this meaning evidences and this meaning and one two, stay there and one two, stay there one stay there two, one two. Evidences of there one two. Evidences of one two. The pleasures are equally divided with themselves. As pleasures are equally divided with

97

themselves Emmet Addis the doughboy a pastoral one two, evidence of equally divided one two, stay there equally divided with evidences equally divided one two.
Emmet Addis the Doughboy a Pastoral Part two.
Divided and two, and what and two, and not and two divided and two and through.
Divided and two and through and what and two and divided and two and divided and two and through.
Emmet Addis the Doughboy a Pastoral Part two.
And through.
Emmet Addis the Doughboy a Pastoral Part two.
Emmet Addis the Doughboy a Pastoral Part two and through.
Emmet Addis the Doughboy a Pastoral Part two.
Going to and as going to, going to and going to and through, going to and through as going to as through. Going to as through and going to, and going to and through.
Emmet Addis the Doughboy.
Emmet Addis and going through.
Emmet Addis and going to.
Emmet Addis and through.
Emmet Addis the Doughboy a Pastoral.
Emmet Addis the doughboy a pastoral part two.
Even as Emmet Addis a pastoral part two.
Not repeat it even an Emmet Addis a Pastoral part two.
Even an not repeat it even an Emmet Addis a Pastoral part two.
Even an not repeat it even an Emmet Addis a doughboy a Pastoral even an Emmet Addis a pastoral part two.
Even an not repeat it even an Emmet Addis even an Emmet Addis a doughboy a Pastoral part two.

Settled as to standing Emmet Addis a doughboy a Pastoral part two. Settled as to standing hire fire part two, settled as to standing Emmet Addis a doughboy a pastoral part two, settled as to standing Emmet Addis a Pastoral part two, settled as to standing Emmet Addis even an Emmet Addis a Pastoral part two. Settled as to standing Emmet Addis a doughboy a Pastoral part two.

Part two settled as to standing not repeat settled as to standing even an Emmet Addis a doughboy part two.

Not repeat, there even an part two, not repeat there, settled as to standing part two, even an Emmet Addis part two settled as to there part two, even an Emmet Addis a Pastoral part two, settled as to there part two, Emmet Addis a doughboy part two settled as to there Emmet Addis part two settled as to standing Emmet Addis even an as to standing part two as to standing a Pastoral even an a doughboy even an settled as to standing even an Emmet Addis a doughboy settled as to standing even an a Pastoral part two settled as to standing Emmet Addis part two.

Not to addition, him from that and not in addition, him from that and in not in addition and in and in from that and him, and him from that and in addition and in addition and in addition in from that. Not in addition him from that not in addition in from that. Not in addition not in addition Emmet Addis not in addition in from that. In addition in from that Emmet Addis in from that in addition in from that in addition. Emmet Addis and not in not in addition not in addition from him, from him and that, in addition not in addition, Emmet Addis not in from that, not in addition not in, from in from that, not in addition from in from that.

A Pastoral Part two to Emmet Addis part two a Pastoral part two Emmet Addis a doughboy a Pastoral part two,

99

part two a Pastoral part two Emmet Addis a pastoral Emmit Addis a doughboy a Pastoral part two.

Not numbers, as not numbers, as not numbers now and there and as not now and there and as not numbers. As not numbers and as not numbers and as not numbers now and as not numbers now and as not now and there and as not numbers and as not now and there and as not numbers. Now and there.

Emmet Addis a pastoral and as not numbers and Emmet Addis a pastoral and as not numbers and as a pastoral now and there and as not numbers and Emmet Addis a doughboy a pastoral now and there and as not numbers.

Emmet Addis a Doughboy a Pastoral now and there and as not numbers a Pastoral part two and Emmet Addis a doughboy a Pastoral part two, and as not numbers and Emmet Addis and now and there and now and there. Emmet Addis a pastoral a Doughboy Emmet Addis a doughboy a Pastoral part two.

This makes having it and having it had it, it had it, this makes having it and having it had it, this makes having it this makes having it had it, this makes having it this makes having it had it. As Emmet Addis as Part two. As Emmet Addis and part two as Emmet Addis as Part two this makes having it this makes having it having it had it.

He can do he can do three things before that and he can do and he does do and he does do as he can do three things before that. This three things before that.

He can do three things he can do three things before he can do that thing not in that order.

Emmet Addis and not in that order Emmet Addis can do three things before that and not in that order, Emmet Addis a Doughboy a Pastoral Part two can do three things before he does that and not in that order. Emmet Addis a Doughboy a Pastoral Part two and not in that order three things before that thing and not in that order.

Finally find it finally not find it finally not find it there finally find it not there and three things before that thing and not in that order and finally find it and finally not find it, and finally not find it there and finally find it not there and he can do three things before that thing and not in that order. Finally find it finally find it not there finally not find it finally three things finally three things before that thing finally find it not there finally not in that order finally find it finally not find it finally find it not there.

Emmet Addis has it carefully and not left so, he has not had it left so he has had it carefully he has carefully had it, he has had it not left so he has had it he has carefully had it he has had it not left so, Emmet Addis has had it not left so a Pastoral Part two, Emmet Addis a Doughboy a Pastoral Part two he has had not left so, he has carefully had it he has carefully had it he has it not left so he has finally not left so he has had not left so he has carefully not left so he has carefully had it not left so he has carefully had it, he has carefully had it not left so he has finally had it not left so he has finally had it he has finally had it not left so. Emmet Addis the Doughboy a Pastoral Part two, he has finally not left it, he has carefully not left so he has had it not left so he has carefully had it he has finally carefully had it he has finally carefully not had it, left so.

Emmet Addis the second part Emmet Addis a pastoral the second part Emmet Addis the Doughboy Part two Emmet Addis a pastoral The Doughboy part two.

Emmet Addis when he was a week, Emmet Addis the Doughboy a pastoral Part two, Emmet Addis when he was a week, Emmet Addis the Doughboy a pastoral part two when he was a week, Emmet Addis the Doughboy a pastoral part two.

Emmet Addis when he was a week, Emmet Addis a doughboy a pastoral part two.

This week, when he was a week, Emmet Addis a Pastoral a doughboy Emmet Addis a Doughboy a pastoral part two when he was a week.

Settlements fairly fairly where there are settlements, where there are settlements fairly where there are settlements when he was a week, fairly where there are settlements where there are settlements fairly a week, fairly a week, Emmet Addis a week.

Fairly where there are settlements fairly Emmet Addis fairly a doughboy fairly a doughboy fairly where there are settlements.

Emmet Addis a doughboy a pastoral part two fairly where there are settlements fairly where there are settlements fairly.

Fairly a week.

If as if as if as seen, if as if as if as if as seen, if as if as if as seen, if as if if as if as if seen. If as if if as if as seen.

Fairly Emmet Addis a doughboy fairly if as Emmet Addis if as Emmet Addis a doughboy a Pastoral, if as if as if as Emmet Addis if as if as if a doughboy as if Emmet Addis as if a doughboy as if Emmet Addis a doughboy a Pastoral.

If as if as if if as if if as if as seen, if as if, fairly Emmet Addis a doughboy a Pastoral if as if fairly as if.

If as if.

Emmet Addis if as if, a doughboy if as if, Emmet Addis a doughboy if as if, fairly seen Emmet Addis a doughboy fairly seen, if as if a Pastoral a doughboy if as if Emmet Addis if as if, fairly seen if as if a doughboy a Pastoral if as if a doughboy a Pastoral Part two if as if Emmet Addis fairly seen a doughboy Emmet Addis a doughboy a Pastoral part two.

If as if seeing to seeing too if as if as seeing to, as seeing to, as seeing to and so not so as seeing to and seeing to and so and seeing to not so and seeing to. And seeing to not so, settlement fairly so and seeing to and seeing to and not so settlement and fairly so and seeing to and seeing to not so and settlement and fairly so, Emmet Addis fairly so and seeing to and fairly so and settlement and fairly so and seeing to and not so and fairly so and seeing to and settlement and fairly so. Not so and fairly so and seeing to, Emmet Addis a doughboy a pastoral and seeing to and not so and settlement and seeing to and fairly so and seeing to and not so and fairly to and seeing to seeing to and fairly to and seeing to and fairly to and not so and fairly to and seeing to and seeing to and not so and seeing to and settlement and fairly to. Fairly to and not so, seeing to and fairly to and settlement and fairly to and seeing to and seeing so and fairly to and seeing to not so and seeing to. Fairly to, seeing to, Emmet Addis a doughboy a Pastoral and seeing to and fairly to and settlement fairly to and seeing to and not so and seeing to and fairly to. And not to and seeing to Emmet Addis a doughboy Emmet Addis and not so and seeing to and fairly to and not so and seeing to and not so and fairly so and seeing to.

17.

Woodrow Wilson

First Scene. Not a dream
                            Not a drama.
First Scene
The birth of Wilson.
In the shadow of our brother we have eaten.
He begins to grow tall.
We cannot neglect youth.
Here we have Woodrow Wilson born in the state of Michigan.
Woodrow Wilson was born in Virginia.
                            First Memory.
I can call.
                            Second Memory.
See the Scene.
                            Third Memory.
I can recollect another thing.
                            Fourth Memory.
My literary digest
                            Second Scene.
Accuse me I accuse myself of earnestness of appreciation of reason and of learning. I do not vary in growth. I am not torn by age. How young am I.
This was said when he was very young. In a minute.
In a moment he was heartily immersed in the very necessary process of illusion and reason and teaching and surveying. Do not neglect persecution. All language is evil.

If you can think that towns are not relieved by growth and if you do believe heartily smile. I can see why humanity is merry. All songs are not songs and all country is not winsome.

In youth we nurse.

Did he emerge then. He did and we do not credit the moment when one may be tall. There are different youths. Some grow tall. All are tall. In some there is no succession of it at all.

The scene of the future. Can you wish that jelly, can you wish that jelly. Can you wish that jelly can be eaten with cream.

The sense of the past.

When they are young they can see that the world is around. Believe me before them.

Consider matters.

The happiness of the future.

This is very funny.

Nodding not nodding together. He grew strong and was not restless nor fearless. He learned that realisation was personality. Can you see to see.

Rest yet.

In speaking to steal singularly men singling men do not frighten them, boys and men plenty of them, we do not speak to steal their hearts away. We reflect the measure of our thought so we are taught and those of us who steal, who can steal. Who can steal from me. Immediately there was a reference to the willingness of all to be willing to go and wait. We wait together. We wait the curse there is no curse for me.

Intermission.

It is singular how conversation can only exist between

Caroline and kitchen.

Youth.

What did youth mean to the Victorian.

Youth is strangely not earnest not abusive not represented and not nearly softened.

I can remember a minister.

How many daughters has each.

Three.

And which is the eldest.

Wood.

And the second.

Forest.

And the third.

Column.

In this way we are not always married.

Mr. Woodrow Wilson comes in or the day.

There is a singular fertility in he recognises. There is a singular fashion in early meaning. Do not mean to be seen.

He was not oblivious of the moon or of noon.

Indeed he had security enough.

In being young we are witnesses.

A drama of life.

Can you believe that he is interested.

Sandwich, Massachusetts, Sandwich glass is made in Sandwich Massachusetts, it was made in Sandwich Massachusetts it was pink and white and often had the form of a dolphin. The dolphin had no connection with the dauphin of France.

Wilson, Mrs. Wilson, we have met a Mrs. Wilson. She is not the wife of the president nor in any way connected with his family.

In English idiom we have an English idiom we have an American phrase, we were astonished to know. America is rarely not represented. We were astonished to know this about education.

He did well in developing.

Hear again.

We do need new subjects

And yet democracy

Who says democracy

Who sings to him.

Who sings to him to-day

Who sings to him to-day soon.

I know how he feels and remains in there out there out of there there he is there.

I can say.

I have learned to pray.

He was always infectuous.

Coming to the weather

If you were born in winter and had your birthday in summer. If you are old in autumn and had your spring altogether, if you were earnestly wishing that ease was outside and that glances and stores and windows and rubber were all useless and prayers were addressed to you how would you answer.

He answered them.

Can you speak to republics.

Can you tell them that you wish them to understand that the old is too old and the new is too old.

Can you tell them this bliss.

Can you tell them that this is the meaning of blessing. Can you really feel silence.

Can you be more solemn than serious more earnest than flagrant. Can you really have been willing.

He has been in the past thirty and forty years of age.

School men.

Encounter him.

Whose was the last diploma that he signed.

Norman

Norman.

The way to think about it is this. Americans can write better English. Americans can express the language. Americans are not surprised to read the phrase outstanding and withstanding and understanding and reasoning. They easily grasp sentences. They do more, they express themselves in English. How can a language alter. It does not it is an altar.

Many play but none play louder.

He was restive and resolute he reasoned and he returned. He was not the one who misunderstood ages the ages of students.

A victory.

The woods the poor man's overcoat.

In seeming, can you say that no interference can be made to-day. Deceive no one, ask for a picture and give it that way. And what is the reward. That it is not presented. That it is not presented. Deceive me. A great many believe in photographs and so he worried for another. Do you believe that fish live and swim above jewels. Many fish swim above jewels. The presented fish swims above the jewels.

Jewels are uncut and pink.

Green and yellow in colour.

Amber and lavender.

So many freezing breaths.

A sound is their sound.

Can wisdom be curtained.

Can choice be necessary.

And now for history.

And now for a history.

History is told and the rest is to unfold and the rest is to be retold and the rest leaves us cold, and history is to be told and a great many scold and say it is told, history is told, will he be a great man will he learn to fan, can fanning be fun, can we satisfy a nun, can we seize what is won can a tall man hold a gun, can a nephew be done can an uncle season, can history be told, will history be told will a history be told can a third party hold, was the last man celebrated, was the first man related, can history can that history be told can we certainly hold our causes together and women's feather, can there be a strange tether when a kingdom can measure, we can measure a treasure, we can treasure a measure. The history is told of a butter and cheese sold. It can be sold for much, a great many can touch, a great many can reflect such a deception. One can be astonished to learn.

Seize easily colonels and kernels.

Did I spell nuts.

Languages.

A rhythm is roused.

Let us languish in thought. Can willing surprise us.

How can you break a chin a chair or an hour glass.

Call me mother.

I call you my mother with all reverence.

I can not doubt that Eugene believes, I cannot doubt that Eugene believes that dizzy that he dizzily believes, that he does dizzily believe, that he believes, where he believes.

All names are changed on roads.

Leaves.

A great many leaves are stated. And govern or govern me there. Any one knows courses. Courses are given in universities. Thinking is done in schools. Justice is done in examples, and privates are more honourable than horses. A great many people love horses.

I wish I knew as much.

No middle life.

When you are lead by the head when you are lead by the street when you are lead by a fork that sings, when you are lead by a bird when you are led by a third, when you are lead to bed, can you seize houses. No one has a pet. A great many pets are sacrificed to shoes.

Shoes and ostrich shoes and ostriches are eaten by women. Men prefer salmon and cod-fish and breasts of ducks and pigeon. Call me a cab sir. A great many thoughts are cold. Is it cold to-day.

Can you say what you do mean by yesterday.

Crowds of witnesses.

We witness that we are patient and seldom taught to swim. A great deal of swimming is bold.

Can you love a couplet.

Mountains of joy.

Glasses are asses. And what passes. Fountains and glasses and water in masses. And masses or ton or a ton is won. And all of it said, that we were not instead, we were not instead of rubbish.

Nobody is particularly inclined to be always industrious.

Can you believe that oceans deceive.

Was he or was he not impressed.

Expressive.

To be expressive is reasonable and to be easily killed is to be easily told that character is predatory. How can you reason about that.

What do you say.

How can you reason about that.

Beseech me, beseech me to love you.

All pearls.

All pearls are rosy and mad, all drink is water and pure, all sorrow is wistful and wrong, all bewilderment is recognised and influential.

Palms, palms are up, palms are held by palms. Palms are grown with palms.

Palms are selected for palms, love is not protected by charms. There is no harm in rhythm.

Poles.

Poles are so tall that they are flag poles.

Wishes are strings.

Words are shocks.

Silver is mellow and riches, no one is richer than his mother. Mother mother come to me and say riches can be sought in every way. Wonder and delight is fine, so is moonlight and sunshine.

Every one is earnest in earnest.

War in peace.

A great many suggest missions. I need admission.

War.

Or what do you say.

Forward enough forward enough forward enough information.

Accomplishment.

To accomplish pins one needs gold. To accomplish sermons one needs letters. To accomplish puddings one needs plains, to accomplish birds one needs water.

To accomplish wishes one needs one's lover.

Can you love another mother. A great many people sing. Not so lightly.

Applause.

When a baby sings and the baby is a boy, he sings seriously and at length. He understands frowning and order and he means to avoid comedy. Comedy is certain certain to be a curtain.

Climb single ropes.

A rope and red ribbon.

How prettily silk and cotton resemble.

And linen who grows linen.

Applause.

Great applause is applause.

Afternoon.

In the afternoon and evening there is a medley of hearing and having. Halving can be pronounced in the same way.

Language.

Can you insert boats.

Ships and boats.

Can you cross and recross, can you cross letters can you cross the letter t.

Means of address.

Read the reason of the blame. I do not blame you for that. I do not blame you because of this. Can you fasten stamps. Can you attach stamps to an envelope. Can you address mail. Can you mail an address. May we be winning.

Right angles.

The right angle is the one that makes a square. Let us regard the square. Let us express regard for the square. The square has many names, circles and acute angles and other indications. He indicated me. I am easily aroused by description, neglect and resolution. Please me repeatedly. How easily do we search.

Wooded Princeton.

Cyprus, Holly, sylvan cellars. Curls, curly is dead.

Rewards.

Breathing is some reward.

Pleasures.

Reading everything again is one of many pleasures.

Troubles.

It is a great annoyance to have so many wishes. I wish to excel. Very well. Very well.

Smiling.

How often do we smile at one another. I spread heartily.

Earnestness.

We were pleased to know that professions are not alike. Many professions differ in detail.

Wells, wells are no longer used with buckets. We now emphasise heat.

Peace.

We colour peace.

Peace altogether.

Is it rash, is it rash to be impulsive and to neglect impulses and to restrain hours. Hours and hours mean depth and do you deride flying, fly and fly and see the children mingle with the coats how much wool is cautious. We are naturally cautious. Can you see shape and obliquity. Can you recall others. Can you sweeten the air. Can you smile to gathering in the honesty of bloom. Bloom bloom away. Smile to freedom.

Extension.

To extend is easily fitted fitted in with me.

Colours, blinded by colours, a negro not a tree, a white soldier or birth, a daring Indian or a real Asiatic, can Lenin silence Lenin, and be vicious, be very delicious. Be very capable of inheritance.

End in singing.

When you make an ending you end the ending by realising that no truth is repeatedly read. Read my candlesticks, lamps and buildings, read my edition in a car. Going from

San Francisco and Oregon and leaving out all who won any and all of us are pleased to say leaves, leaves are dry, grass grass is wet, creeks creeks are rushing and birds birds whistle.

Whistle and I'll come to you my lad.

18.

Or More (or War)

The American people during the American civil war. What did they go to war for and who went to the war. The American people during any war during a war any people during a war during any war a war any war during a war, during any war a people during any war or a war.
Carefully.
Did they like the war, did they like any war did they like any war. Carefully.
He had and they did not they did find it put away.
They had and very nearly when it was larger and never larger and smaller.
They had when at once when at once and at once.
Accustomed to it.
And at once in glasses.
This has no meaning strangely.
Once twice and at once. At once and once. At once once twice and at once.
At once.
At once once and twice at once. At once and twice. At once. Once.
Always it they went and there and there and as much. As much and carefully.
Carefully makes an example and an interest in white and smaller. White and smaller and smaller and as if fortunately. Fortunately carefully. Carefully.

In their place and in place of it. Would it make any difference if water if water was water. Was it.
Or for.
Early and late.
The war is as early.
Or the war is as early.
This is this and this is this about it. This is this about it.
After or before a war.
Early and late and in this way and in this way, this is this this is this and this and this and this and this and as much.
Or more.
To add to the war.
When the ones who have who have who have it here and and there.
They go you go Hugo Hugo you go they go.
Carefully.
It is intended that in place of it all who meet with having added and particularly, would he would he and would he, and an article. An article is in use.
Carefully.
This is needed for it this is needed for it said it.
War or, or for, or more, or more and listen.
Listen best and listen next and listen.
Having forgotten that she went there.
Having forgotten that he went there.
Having forgotten.
Having forgotten carefully.
The american people during the american civil cuban Mexican indian and European war. No other war was a war.
If no other war was a war if no other war was a war what did they feel was a war when there was a war.
The people of America when there was a war.

Nightly at night.
And needed to be astonished by, and because, of it, by it and because of it, with them.
Carefully.
Carefully and misuse.
And this is an opening.
Which best.
Which is best.
Which is the best.
Which is which which is best which is the best.
Appealing to themselves, themselves, appealing to themselves, appealing to them, to them, appealing to them, to themselves appealing to themselves.
War seldom.
Wars as seldom.
As seldom as wars.
As seldom.
Wars as seldom.
That there are wars as seldom, that they as seldom that they are wars as seldom as wars.
Carefully as seldom, as seldom, as seldom too as seldom as seldom to, as wars as seldom as wars.
Wars are as seldom.
Nouns and not, not and nicely, nicely and as nicely.
The people of the United States, who said the people of the United States seldom and seldom and advised.
Advisable.
Carefully and advisable.
In no one in no one in one in no one and in use and in no one and in no one and in use, and in, use and no one and in use.
In use and no one and in use.
What causes what.
The cause of it is this. Having heard of something and some

one who was and might be and perhaps might relax and not be as it was nearly in comfort and necessarily comfortably having heard of some one was it possible to decide as quickly. It would have been if there had not been at first a discovery, second an advance in relations and thirdly a delight in decision. No one is delightful to some, some and some, sum and sum and sum. Delightful.

Delightful and carefully and a pleasure.

In this way would a mother prefer a nephew or a father.

When the people of the United States have stationed and stationed themselves when they have stationed themselves. Gracious and ungracious disturbed and undisturbed.

Delightfully and carefully and a pleasure.

The meaning of war is this war and the meaning of war is this, the meaning of war is this, and the meaning of war and the meaning of war is this.

In beginning to mention objects.

In order.

War in order in order and beginning to mention, to mention war in order to begin to mention in order, war in order and as pleased and as pleasure and as pleasure and as pleased. If he said that if they said that changed that to that and apply, apply for it.

Too, and new, new and new and too.

Quickly ended at once.

Quickly ended at once at once and new, at once.

At once and as quickly and as quickly ended.

What does he mean when he says that it is not possible he being a man whose training has made him capable of arranging one thing and that thing being something that has been needed in a way needed needed in a way would any one believe that he could see just as well.

Easily pleased.

City is short for citadel.
To tell.
Do tell.
To tell.
To tell all about it.
Do tell.
Do tell all about it that city is short for citadel.
Inspired by a minute.
That city is short for citadel is what there is to tell.
Do tell that city is short for citadel inspired by a minute that city is short for citadel.
When war is fortunately when more is fortunately when more is fortunately, when war is fortunately more is fortunately war is fortunately war is fortunately, more and war fortunately more fortunately war. When war is more fortunately, when more fortunately when war fortunately when war when more fortunately.
It is easier to guess than to guess.
It is as easy to guess yes as to guess.
It is as easy as to guess yes. It is as easy as that to guess yes as easily as to guess yes as to guess yes as to guess that. It is as easily as to guess. As to guests, it is as easy it is easily, it is as easy, easily, and this in advance, and around, around it.
Who knows, what what and there, he knows, what and there, and he knows what and what and what and there.
Carefully.
Always connected to carefully.
He goes, he goes when he is sent.
When he comes, how many differences are there.
Differences are differences between when he and when he does.
Consider it as war.
In the beginning consider it more.

In the beginning, if they that is if he, if we and they and he if we and if he frequently there are one and two.

And more.

Another trouble and another trouble.

Meet and met.

Does she want more.

She does.

The people of America go out and come in. The people of America during and before and afterwards have heard and have heard it.

The people of America have been satisfied with what has been noticed during before and after a war.

A war and again.

A war and again.

More and not more and not again and not again.

Coming down stairs.

Carefully.

To see.

He thought it was made.

Because they always have it there.

He thought it was made because they always have it there. If everything has had it, has had it, later and if everything, if everything, has had it, if everything has had it later and as early.

Two times two.

Four times two.

Four times two.

Two times too.

Two times too.

Carefully.

Four times two.

As carefully.

They had as they had they had had as they had had. They

had had as they had had, as they had had, as they had had.
Two times two.
As carefully two times two times two.
More than as long.
More then more then in more then, or more then or more then, or more.
More too.
When they were the people of the United States before during and after and before war.
How do I know how many there are without counting. Count four. How many there are. Four and a chair, four and open. To open and open, to open into three, open four open into three and there, there, just there, open it there, not with care not carefully. It serves as a rest.
Who calls it lower.
They do.
Who knew what to call it.
They did not.
Who liked it.
Everybody liked it.
Who liked it better.
Everybody liked it better.
Who liked it best.
Everybody liked it best.
Who knew what to call it.
It is really in a way larger, and as large as suits them, it is in a way just what it is. Can it open. It can if it is open. When it is open as openly as it is open, open open, and on it, a lamp an ink-well and a pencil. In this way in war and in peace.
Everybody knows another not another like it. Everybody knows another like it not another like it. Everybody knows another like it not another like it.

To remind that the people of the United States before afterward during and at war.

She said no not if she could.

After that there was general conversation.

She said she as certainly would and would she, may be she would but I doubt it.

After this, and as much more and as much more that was not eaten.

Can any one think that if the whole of the country, what in a way as a whole if in a way as a whole and this country, if in a way as a whole and this or that or the country of that, that is a country.

A country is very nearly plainly to be seen.

Here and there.

A country is an express train after express trains are used.

Can anybody remember all of a plate.

A plate is unique.

So is it in effect.

In effect and ineffective.

Flowers in relation and for relations.

I did not say roses.

He said roses.

I did not say pansies.

He said pansies.

I did not say colours.

He said colours.

I did not say hats.

He said hats.

This makes it appear to be helped.

All who mention more.

All who mention war.

All who mention war.

All who mentioned war.

The people of the United States all who mentioned the people of the United States all who mentioned the people of the United States before during and after, all who mentioned the people of the United States all who more than that all who mentioned more than that all who mentioned more than that more than that the people of the United States during before and after war, during war after war during and after and before war, more all who mentioned the people of the United States before during and after during and after during and after and before during and after and during and before and afterwards. Afterwards in mentioned and afterwards.

These are the different things that have been attended to. This has been attended to that has been attended to, that has been attended to, this has been attended to. These are the different things that have been attended to.

Who makes miles, miles as miles. Who makes as many miles as many miles as as many miles. Who makes as many miles and who makes as many miles, more at least, more at once, more at most, more or less.

Who makes as many cups as there are cups. Who makes as many as ever.

Who makes who makes it do.

It happened in this way.

After every other other one, after every other one after after every after every other one and as round.

Round makes it useful. Useful makes it in reason, and in reason or a reason or with reason or belief. Believe me it is not for pleasure that I do it.

An advantage to him and to them.

In actual measurement or more.

When a carelessly attracted canal canal and river or, or as much as from there to there, can and can and can it have

a man and a man stores and if to know it went. Went away.
He went away to stay.
So briefly does it mean that unexpectedly unexpectedly
why and shy.
Do nearly, nearly nearly too, to do, a great to do. Care-
fully.
Who has forgotten who has forgotten forgotten, forgotten
what.
Animals.
Animals are left.
Birds.
Birds are left.
Towels.
Towels are left.
Butter.
Butter is left.
Who has forgotten, forgotten, forgotten what.
Any one can say that at once.
Why was he nervous.
When three men see another then, when three men see then
see then do they separate into two and two into two and one
and then one then two then two then one then two then
two one two then one is one then do they separate then do
they around then do they separate then and around then
and surround then and two then and one then.
Why is he nervous.
A little later nearly later than that. This makes more
oftener. Having never forgotten him. He liked this liked
that liked that liked this.
How much influence have they. Did he know about it.
Pretty quickly too. This they knew. This they knew.
Pretty quickly too.
Once twice three times four times, four times three times,

once twice three times, once twice three times four times, four times three times three times once twice three times once twice three times four times, four times once twice three times.

Joining unexpectedly.

Have to be carefully.

All at once or all at once more all at once more all at once or or all at once or all at once more all at once or more or all at once.

War makes a cousin, a cousin a cousin a cousin. War makes a cousin. War makes a cousin. War makes a cousin a cousin.

Happy to have war.

It is a very extraordinary thing that as it happens one who has had an opportunity to sit recognises them just the same. In the first place to clean, in the second place to place in the third place to nicely very nicely follow. She is pretty nearly.

Who could think of going across across. Now listen to what she says, she says she heard saw and was fastidious, in this and in this way and she meant, she meant to have it happen, the first time a message, a second time a message and a third time a message, a message and a messenger and a messenger and what. What does she say. She says that if she says not again, and not again and if she says, if she says how do you do this, and how do you do, if she says that she has probably, if she says she probably and she very, and she very perfectly and as she has to try to correct, correct correctly, in places and places, in that respect a division is just like a division, it is just like a division it is just like and as it is just like as it is just like a division, a division makes a difference. A difference to what and further, further it pleases, it pleases, where it pleases, where it pleases, as a pleasure, as a pleasure, a pleasure for the plates and the plates, plates and very nearly attract her, and very nearly attract her and for and very nearly and for and very nearly attractive. This is one of the cases and not either before or after. Before and after makes it do the what makes it do the what and not what and not what and not what and the dinner. Before and after has for these reasons, for their descriptions for their attractions, for their reductions. Who knows every once in a while and who knows it better because of itself and and no one ever mentions either it either.

She did mention 54 and six, she did mention have to have it mix she did mention little halves at once she did mention it finally. And at last. At last they said what should be said first at last, what should be said at first. Nobody knows how many times how many times at hand at hand. Have to have heard it said. Suitable and said.

She needs she needs to a last afternoon after war. After war is he after war.

Fell at once felt at once felt at once fell at once.

How do they know that how do they know that they are astonished how do they know that they are astonished in this way how do they know that that they are astonished in this way at once at first at once, and once and at once.

How do they know that they are astonished at once.

Do they need to count forty-five to know that there are forty-five there do they need to count more than forty-five to know that there are more than forty-five there do they need to count less than forty-five to know that there are less than forty-five there.

The people of the United States have been before have been after and have been before and after and have been after and before and have been more have been more after and before and have been before a war and have been after and before and a war. The people of the United states have been before and after and more before and more after and have been before. Have the people of the United States been before and after and at war. Have the people of the United States have they ever have they ever been at war before. A great many questions asked and answered.

Five whites make six roses, six roses make three whites, three whites make five pinks five pinks make four everywhere.

This is in case of war.

Who knows best. They do.

She says that it would please them.

When and when did they, when did they and when. When and when and when did they. We have refused three at once and accepted one hundred and thirty. We have accepted one hundred and thirty and we have refused three at once.

How often have and has a movement a movement of paper paper moving been considered interrupting and finally. Finally to be funny. Funny at all.

Funny is a word that has been used and has not been used. When it was used when it was in use when it was not in use when it is not. When it is not and not found. Found and funny both not in use when and when and when not and when in use not in use. This makes more, this makes more this makes more and more and in in precedes an, an and in and on and also. Also found in use an occasion on account. Incapacitated.

Finish and furnish and war and more. War and more and fasten and find. Find and felt and fitted as well. Do suddenly suddenly do suddenly. Having had to hold Harry. Harry can also be called Henry or more.

The people of the United States and dreamed about them.

He stated this about those. Which is and chose. Fortunately at that.

Let me make a statement. It is this. To be aroused because he was the only one. To refuse not to refuse but to decline. To be and she had helped and this is for them not a mistake because otherwise to arrange it for them. Listen to war. He and she were helpful.

What makes it smell as if an orange was burnt and if an orange is burnt.

Whose and whose and whose, after that whose.

It is very pleasurable that if it is his it is his and if it is theirs it always is theirs and if it is his it always is his. His and his. Finally the difference between more and more. How nearly does it sound alike.

In as well and read to me, past it.

Fortunes are forty times forty times fortunes and fortunes are forty times as fortunes are forty times fortunes.

This makes more and Agnes and it. And reputations fortunately. In this way in this war in their war in the war. Hours and houses and parts of it. Introducing houses introduced parts of it; introducing hours and houses and parts of it. He knew at once.

Not this not that and that and a hat had it is a betrothal and an evaporation that concludes more.

When these made thank you and to mix names. Supposing Jenny and Fanny, supposing Howard and Herbert supposing Isabel and Ida. This makes morning evening afternoon and morning.

After the war.

Did he ask him.

The people of the United States of America before during and after a war. Apart and apart whose was the difference between restlessness and neglect between willing and welling between foolishness and refuse, between too sweet and safely. Having had chairs known to be chairs and simply safely had it in their way and likelihood and before it was at once. He knew how to turn. It is easily seen that at once and fortunately and in their habits.

Having had.

After all.

Were there as many there.

As were there.

After all.

Having had.

Were there as many there as were there.

If he waited, for it.

If he had it, for it.

If he heard it, and it.

If he did and he said, even if he said and even.

They have decided about two days in the week, two sides two, and two sides to hold at the head of at the head of this result.

Forty thousand times three makes one hundred and twenty thousand. The modest sum of ten thousand, ten thousand and seventy thousand. One thousand for each and division. Division calls for colour, colours call for not for.

Kindly mix harmony and history, respect and restoration, inviolable and interested and undertaken and advantage. For the rest as for the rest, at most and satisfied too.

In their case they meant to eulogise and return and relieve, relieve at once. What is the difference between between, between and mean.

An announcement.

He and he was prepared to say that he returned at once.

He and he was attached and definite. He and pleasantly retired and as coming.

Before and after and between war.

The people of the United States of America between after and before war.

Uncles and clouds.

Out loud.

Larger at once.

He knew that in face he knew that in face of it and he knew that in face, in face of it.

Not much.

He heard wholly more.

And then at least at war.

War makes a fish.

Have it.

War makes a dish.

Halve it.

War makes it which.

Which has it.

War makes it which which has it.

After this, war.

Then he had a little way to go and he said so.

Who has held ahead.

Play ahead.

Who has had ahead.

Whether head.

Or whether or whether or ahead.

Will you be pleased to have it.

Not to be not to be not to be not to be exchange it here for a minute. A minute makes no appointment or it. After that at most. Whether and seat and settled makes an origin.

Originally, forty was what they said.

At her and to her and to her and by her, by her and with her and with her and yet.

Yet makes a difference between met.

After this a description.

When after walking and walking is where is it. Where is it might be in that at once hyacinth. Nobody knows mixings and mixed. Mixed and forgotten and freshly she knew that it was that that was repeated. Did she, and did she. She said it was not he was not she was not here.

So much before, so much between, between and after, so much after between and after. So much after. So much between and after. Then came the next.

Now it is all over.

Could he not have said could he not have said.

Never again will there be any connection between any connection between and seen any connection between seen and said so any connection between any connection in between and said so and seen and seen and said so and between and in between and said so and seen.

Having decided the United States having decided the United states and having decided it can be remembered that hereditary can commence in one generation.

Who needs had. Who needs who had who and had in plural.

Never thinking of it and never thinking of it and never any more and never thinking of it any more.

One hand one hand one hand, attracting it to the best, first and best most and best, best and most best and first.

This is a description, two men leaning that is one man leaning that is one man sitting that is one man standing that is one man standing and leaning that is one man sitting and leaning. Parts and parts of it, parts of it very well. Is it more difficult to gesticulate than not. To repeat. They are said to be the same and the next is said at once, as it is when they are here and they must have had it too, two and longer. More.

War is this, this war, war is this and this war and this war. This war makes slate useful and just in this way, a slate when it is rubbed is gray and when it is polished is black this makes unpleasant to the eye and the ear. She said are they scarce and he said they are scarce. He said are they at all scarce and she said they are not at all scarce they are not as scarce and he said they are not as scarce. After that an occasional return.

How can war finish how can a war finish, a war can finish by adding and by adding a war can finish. A war can finish by not adding that a war can finish. A war can finish by adding that by adding that and by adding, a war can finish by adding a war can finish adding. This is not exactly what I said.

Two say, three say, I say I say, I say they say, they say two say, to say you say, you say two say, two say three say I say they say they say I say three say two say. And a war and I finish and I finish and a war. It is a very extraordinary thing that one does not know what one means until one says it, it is also a very extraordinary thing that one says what one means when one has said it, it is a very extraordinary thing that one says it is a very extraordinary thing what one says and it is a very extraordinary thing that what one says that one means what one says and it is a very extraordinary thing that one says that one says it. What does one say. One says one says. And what does one mean. One means what one says when one says it. Does one mean what one says when one says it. Does one say what one says does one. Does one does one exactly and more more is a name.

Hill hill hill, hill hill hill hill hill hill hill gap. As foolish as a lap. And then mistaken. Not at nine.

He originally cultivated tea, he originally cultivated he originally cultivated cows and he originally cultivated it. After that he joined himself to all of them and after that he was as helpful as he could be. This makes more. After that he was nearer and nearer and after that he had had made what was to be attended to. This does make the difference.

Expect to rest just as well expect the rest just as well to expect and to rest as well to rest as well to expect to rest to rest as well to expect it as well.

After that he attended to everything and after that he attended to everything and after that he had attended to everything.

You know how soon.

I asked her if she would care to go. No, she said no. I told her I told her so I told her how I know and I told her that so and so and so and so and she said it was just as well. In this way they had to begin to count. Is any one annoyed when they begin to count. In this way after and before.

If he knew certainly that an elephant is small and an elephant is small if he knew certainly that an elephant is small and if he knew certainly that an elephant is small and attaching who makes ministers. Ministers is a way of saying how do you do.

Let us consider the question of war. As has often been said as it is and as it has often been said the people of the United States before during and after a war, as it has been said the people of the United States as it has been said during before and after a war.

This makes me happen to have to be sweeter. And not changed.

Not at all not at all not at all.

Stop there stop here and there to stop here and there not at all to stop here and there. To stop here and there.

Who knew who knew Caroline.

At first at once at least.

When actually in case and in an accident useful use of them you will.

Play to treasure, I do.

Play to play to I do.

In twenty times in twenty-eight, in twenty-eight in eight, hurry up hills. After that it was almost all the time. Now then seriously.

Likes to be sweet.

Likes to eat.

Likes to likes to likes to likes to.

As likes to be sweet.

Just as likes to be sweet.

That is one reason. Find it.

Jump they used to say jump and they used to say it is vertical horizontal practical and long. They come together and apart and they are reunited.

Height can be the same as equal.

To then that is the reason to their again then to then that is the reason again then to then, again then. That is the reason that if it holds it would if it holds it would. It would if it holds.

How many make five different. Counted correctly five different, how many make five different counted correctly make five different.

Only a habit.

If it is so sweet to see if it is so very sweetly, if it is to see so very sweetly, if it is very sweetly to see, see and saw, he saw. After that was it. Never again will he remember will he remember that they are of no use to him.

It is very well to say every day. It is is it is it is it. And say every day. Two who are women and two who are women are two. Then comes, did it interfere. After at once and looking as if it had been nearly there. All of it made it.

Did they did they go did they go indigo did they go had they gone had they gone here. Here and here. At least there were.

Not at all as well.

There is no more no more there are no more hats. There are no more hats there. There are plates and plates and plates plates of it.

She need never be mentioned.

Surprise for surprise.

You surprise we surprise and do surprise would be surprised if after all he did a very little one. Would be surprised.

Would be surprised and more would be surprised would be surprised more. Would be surprised war and more. She would not be surprised.

Habit and have it have it and habit.

Attracted to the pin and pin, coral pin.

It is very astonishing that once upon a time there was a blue room and a gold room and a red room and a yellow room. It is astonishing that once upon a time there was a gold room and a blue room and a red room and a rose room. It is astonishing that once upon a time there was a rose room and a gold room and a yellow room and a blue room. It is astonishing that once upon a time there was a gold room and a blue room and a yellow room and a rose room. Three attacks were thrown back and two attacks were vigourously defeated. Two attacks were vigourously defeated and three attacks were thrown back. At once at once who are four at once. We are.

Or so exciting.

Not to stop and not to stay not to stay and not to stop. Stop it.

It is annoying to be told and to be told it is annoying to be told and to be told it is annoying to be told and to be told it is annoying to be told and to be told.

Nobody knows how open and how closed not as well as in another way. Nobody knows how open and how closed nobody knows nobody knows how open and how closed it is. It is. Nobody knows how open and how closed it is. It is.

Would it be thought eight hundred eight hundred and ninety two nine hundred and nine hundred and twenty five and nine hundred and thirty could be taught and would be taught and would be taught and could be taught. Nobody knows. Ask them. Nobody knows ask them nobody knows it would be taught it could be taught. What is it that would be taught. Ask them.

A baby has a hat or two and so do you and so do you if a baby has a hat or two and if so do you and if so do you and if a baby has a hat or two and if so do you.

And if after that he has to have he has to have it.

Let no one say that ten are more and six are more and eight are more let no one say so any more more more war.

Just as pleasantly as that for them.

Let those who will have a bird to-day and see a bird any way and have a bird that way let those who will.

Let us consider the case of Harriet and Henrietta of Herbert of Will and the difference between. After forty years after fifty years after twenty years after eighty years more or less. Poe a study.

No one sees the connection between Lily and Louise but I do.

How are houses. Houses are houses.

It would not be necessary to have an alternative because and this is the reason why, it would not be necessary to have an alternative because if eighty and forty-eight and seventy-six are all as attached to candles no one ever does. Ever does. Ever does has noises.

At once and more.

She was not as pleased with this as with that. She was not.

Let any one absently seize and see, see and be seen and saw and more. This does not make disappointment.

Now we know.

Enthusiastically.

We have at last discovered what to say when and practically plainly and a purse. This is it. Neither once or twice neither three or four, neither four or five. All of them together makes adjoining. Oh so sweetly there. Who can have oranges and grape fruit and grape fruit is larger and oranges are yellower not yellower but more of a colour. This satisfies union and strength. Let us every one wish. This is what to think of more.

More is a name.

Yes sir.

More is a name.

Yes sir.

Yes sir More is a name.

Let each one reply about fruits.

Fruits are apples pears peaches oranges plums and dates.

After that there is no annoyance.

Does anything confuse you.

No nothing does.

After that cordially yours.

Come back comfortably to more.

Is comfortably come back. Is comfortably come back comfortably to more, comfortably to more, come back comfortably to more. To more. Comfortably come back to more.

He does not mention it either and as however however is as either. This makes a war a seat of war. No one knows how many days there are in it. If did anybody say if, if and they use houses if and they use uses it does not make it as it was said. What was said. Butter and noise was said. What was said. Butter and both was said. What was said. Butter and both and butter was said. What was said. Butter and both and butter and both was said. What was said. Butter and both was said.

Let them name everything.

The first thing the first thing is to say there were two children. The second thing is to say there were two children. The third thing is to say there were two children. Two children are each one one. One and one makes two. Two makes one and one. One and one makes two. Two makes it as bewitching. Who places doors. Doors are made after to-day and before to-day, and it is easy to say afterwards, we know what was not to his credit. In this way. Supposing we had met any day and we had liked. He would want to know how much it was and we we would be very pleased and we would arrange and some one would tell me not at all, and she was right.

That makes one.

Supposing we did meet and he would like to have heard it.

He did hear it and why because we said it and by this and very likely he knew too. This makes it at once and this time he said it and fortunately who has who has who has sometimes all the time and this makes more than two it makes two too. Who has ahead had ahead.

I have never heard her say it.

What either or neither.

This makes more and not for before.

In San Francisco they have fog at night.

This makes it have three names, Gertrude, Henry and Celestine.

In this way they have it as it is alright and partially pleased.

You will never be angry with Ida.

At once more.

So soothingly.

This is the way it has to be. It has to be this is the way and not to do it again.

She has absolutely promised never to mention birds.

Every one promises a day. And now to act as if it was or if it was. It should have been the other.

It is easy to remain here and not end it.

And supposing they were prepared supposing they were.

When the king wanted to he called each one and he said come at once.

Why as likely he went first.

Having learned to tell it all.

Who was rested first.

And no town mentioned.

Who was mentioned first by themselves.

And they might.

The only nice thing about it is this. He might just as easily not have to have all of it.

139

The only nice thing about money is spending it and so and so if they go and so if they go and they say so what will they inhabit, they will inhabit cities countries and boats.

When in this case they say that they will pay what will they pay they will pay and as in a way Saturday is a day and so is Sunday. This makes tea stronger.

What does more do more makes it take its place, and what does war do war makes mountains mountains and little girls little girls. This has to do with it.

Everybody forgot Friday.

After each one easily.

Count and account.

That is a difference.

The difference stays and who makes and one another.

Even he cannot hesitate.

Connect and disconnect.

Attend and while.

Before and arrangement.

They amounted to it as prettily.

Who makes a mistake, not at all, who intends to leave home not at all. Who intends to be so sweet. No one should mix dinner and butter so they say.

She says she knew that this was true.

Not liking to have defeat said to be said to be if fortunately a reason.

There are two days in which to have or to have or to have and these are more attaching. She wrote and said that she did not wish to see what had been said. No answer. She wrote and said that she did not wish to know what she had said she wrote and said that she did not wish to know what she had said. This makes it happily attached to the best that has been written and said and very good now. Now and how and have to allow him to come for them. This makes bells and eggs and two. Too too too many say so now too too too many too. Too too too many say so now so many say so too. Who to, to whom and to, too many say so now too too many too.

This makes hay on the road and one behind the other. How often have they stopped. Just as often.

She was new too to it.

I have a way to say a day a day to say a day to-day he has to too. This makes it an effort for them to continue to attach attachments to it. It is very seldom and very foolish and well remembered to know that they do grow and in that way noises and noiselessly and in between. How very seldom and exchange. In exchange.

He said that he wanted to know and at length at length and he wanted to know forget how it sounded.

Not interested in war.

More.

Not interested in war.

More.

More and war is different.

Not interested in war.

More.

More and war is different.

To begin and never mention stretching stretching it in that direction. Thank you.

Now to see a pleat.

To-morrow a choice.

To-morrow morning.

She explained that twelve hundred is too much, that eleven hundred and seventy-five is too much that one thousand is just right. Would she kindly beg for more for her, and after that they very well know that she is uneasy. And so they know that they were so. Difference between war and were.

Sweet smiles over apples oranges and figs cut up and on white.

How many seconds are there in war. Twenty seconds. And how many seconds more, not many seconds more. How many seconds are there in war. There are twenty seconds there are in war there are twenty seconds in war there are in war there are more in war there are no more than twenty seconds in war.

Philip six and Philip five, five and wife is the same six and face is the same six and prick is the same five and have is the same, five and thrive is the same six and pick is the same six and held is the same five and share is the same after that inclosed.

Counting pansies is as useful as that, it always is and they do like what they have pretended and intended.

She likes it when she is mentioned and she likes it when she is mentioned. To have very well expected to-morrow and he respects it. After that comes mid-day and after that in two places. Before and more an exactitude. Was she at once. Who has.

Forty-two changes.

Easily.

Begin with forty-one.

Every inch away they say.

Fortunes follow an index.

And in all they changed their mind.

This makes a minute.

Attack appreciatively.

All of this and house.

And so we say and so we have and so we and as will be and as will be too and there.

Attitude to this.

The attitude to this is this. All of it husbands. Husbands

can be used to say husband can be used to say to husband.
Laugh for me.
Who has had it sailours.
Who has had it capturing.
Who has had it sadly.
Who has had it the next day.
Who has had it on and the half was severe was it. Who has
prepared that it did not wholly disappear.
One one and one and decidedly.

19

An Instant Answer or A Hundred Prominent Men

What is the difference between wandering behind one another or behind each other. One wandered behind the other. They wandered behind each other, they wandered behind one another.

Kings counts and chinamen.

A revival.

I will select a hundred prominent men and look at their photographs hand-writing and career, and then I will earnestly consider the question of synthesis.

Here are the hundred.

The first one is used to something. He is useful and available and has an unclouded intelligence and has the needed contact between Rousseau and pleasure. It is a pleasure to read.

The second one and in this case integrity has not been worshipped, in this case there has been no alternative.

The third one alternates between mountains and mountaineering. He has an anxious time and he wholly fails to appreciate the reason of rainfall. Rainfall sometimes lacks. It sometimes is completely absent and at other times is lacking in the essential quality of distribution. This has spread disaster.

The fourth one illustrates plentifully illustrates the attachments all of us have to what we have. We have that and we are worried. How kind of you to say so.

The fifth one of the fifth it has not been said that there have been three told of the gulf stream and the consul.

Frank, where have you been. I have not been to London to see the queen.

The sixth one the sixth one thoroughly a pioneer. He is anchored we do not speak of anchor nor of diving he is readily thoughtful. He has energy and daughters. How often do we dream of daughters. How often. Just how often.

The seventh is mentioned every day.

The eighth. Can you pay the eighth to-day. Can you delay. Can you say that you went away. Can you colour it to satisfy the eye. Can you. Can you feel this as an elaborate precaution. Can you.

The ninth one is vague. Is he vague there where they care to insist. Is he vague there or is he inclined to tease. Is he inclined to tease. We know what we show. A little quarter to eight. I hope you will conduct him to his seat. He does not need politeness. No and he tells you so. No.

The tenth one the tenth one feels traces of terror. This does not sound wealthy nor wise nor does he plan otherwise. He planned very well. There is always this to tell of him. He can be a king or a queen or a countess or a Katherine Susan. We know that name. It has always been the same. At the same time every one shows changes. We arrange this at once.

The eleventh. Who won you. That is very sweet. Who were you. Expected pages and word of mouth, and by word of mouth. Expect pages and by word of mouth. Who won one. Who won won. Mrs. Mrs. kisses, Mrs. kisses most. Mrs. misses kisses, misses kisses most. Who won you.

And the twelfth. The twelfth was the man who restrained Abel and Genoa. Why do the men like names. They like names because they like calling. A calling is something to follow. We no longer represent absence. I call you. Hullo

145

are you there. I have not been as intelligent yet as I was yesterday.

Thirteen, the thirteenth has not neglected the zenith. You know how to invent a word. And so do you. You know how to oblige him with lilacs. And so do you, you know you do. And you know how to rectify an expression. Do you build anew. Oh yes you do.

The fourteenth prominent man is prominent every day of the year. Do you feel this to be at all queer. He is prominent and eminent and he is personally severe. He is not amiable. How can an amiable baby pronounce word. How can they be predominant. We know why we have reason we reason because of this.

The fifteenth is wholly exhilarated. Place air and water where they are.

The sixteenth yes indeed. Have we decreed. Yes indeed. Have we. Do we need that.

The seventeenth. The seventeenth century is older than the sixteenth. How much older. A century older. Or older than a century older. The seventeenth is a century older is older than a century older than the sixteenth.

The eighteenth one wishes to annex the Philippines.

The nineteenth one mingles with men. We say he mixes with men. We say he mixes up nothing. He does not mix things up nor does he do the opposed thing. When he does ring and he does ring, what, that is what he says, what. What does he say. He says what did I say. He says. Did I ring. I say, he says, I say did you say anything. How cleverly brothers mingle. We haven't forgotten.

The twentieth. No one forget anything and he does not forget anything. He does not forget anything when he is here. Does he forget to come again. He does not elaborate exercises. There are witnesses there.

The twenty-first nursed what was to him beaming. I can declare that they are not aware of seeming to share policing. They have increased the number of police in New York.

The twenty-second, how many more days are there in September than there were. This question has been aroused by the question asked by the prominent man who is the subject of the declaration that words may be spoken.

The twenty-third is not indicated by invasion. We all believe that we do invade islands countries homes and fountains. We do believe that the hierarchy of repetition rests with the repeaters. Now we severally antedate the memory. Do you relish powder.

Of the twenty-fourth it has been said that out of sight out of mind is not so blind. Please do not wave me away. Waves and waves they say carry wood away. Carry, does that remind you of anything.

The twenty-fifth is moderately a queen. What did you say. Anger is expressive and so are they.

The twenty-sixth has many ordinary happinesses. He is ordinarily in the enjoyment of his challenge. Do not challenge him to-day. What did you say. Do not challenge him to-day.

The twenty-seventh does measure very well indeed the heights of hills. How high are they when they are negligible. How high are they any way and where do dogs run when they run faster and faster. And why do dog lovers love dogs. Do you know everything about deer. He had a father and they made a window and windows have never been scarce.

The twenty-eighth is perceptibly loving. He has invented perfumes and portraits and he has also reconciled stamina with countenance. I do say that yesterday he was very

147

welcome. And to-day. To-day he is very welcome. We do not say that it is wonderful to be loaned at all.

The twenty-ninth neglects the history of a mute. Mute and unavailing. The twenty-ninth does not add considerably to his expense. He is not needed there. Where is he needed. He is needed here and there. Drive me there.

The thirtieth manages to be lavish. He washes land and water, washes them to be green, wishes them to be clean, his daughter merits her mother and her sister her brother. He himself witnesses this himself and he carries himself by special train. A train of cars. Will there soon be no trains of cars. Did you hear me ask that. Will there pretty soon be no bridling.

The thirty-first remembers that a pump can pump other things than water and because of this he says miles are astray. They have proof of this. Can you solidly measure for pleasure.

The thirty-second is an irresistible pedestrian. He has much choice, he chooses himself and then his brother and then he rides back. He can seem in a dream and he can uncover the lover. I have been so tender to-day.

The thirty-third is incapable of amnesty. Forgive me for that you dear man. Where were you born. I was born in a city and I love the whole land.

The thirty-fourth is second to none in value. Why do you value that more. Why do you value you value that any more.

The thirty-fifth why can there be naturally this one who has found it invigorating to exchange beds for beds and butter for butter. Exchange butter for butter. Do exchange more beds for more beds.

The thirty-sixth has heard of excitement. How can you be

excited without a reason. How can you be an adaptable tenth. He is in the tent. There is a tent there.

The thirty-seventh for the thirty-seventh a great many tell the truth, they tell the truth generously. Somebody is generous there where the rest of them care. Do they care for me. Do they. How awfully popular I am.

The thirty-eighth has held enough and he holds the rest there where there are no more edible mushrooms. Do you know how, to tell an edible mushroom. Have you heard all of the number of ways.

The thirty-ninth is contented and alarmed. Why do you share and share alike and where do you share what you share. What do you care.

The fortieth is rapidly rained on. Rain is what is useful in Europe and not necessary where you have irrigation. Do you understand me. And why do you repeat what you say. I like to repeat what I say.

The forty-first one did he duck. Did he say I wish they would go away, did he describe himself, did he feel that he was married, did he entertain on next to nothing and did he furnish houses and did he candidly satisfy enquiries. Did he learn to quiet himself. Did he resemble ready money and did he inquire where they went. How can all shawls be worn all the time. Some say it is very fine to-day.

The forty-second what did you say, the forty-second came every day and yet how can he come every day when they are away. He comes anyway and he replaces what he uses and he uses it there and he promises to share what he has and he is very prominently there. We stay home every day when he comes here. I don't quite understand, I am a little confused. Does he come every day.

The forty-third one is the one that has inevitably established himself in the location which is the one that was intended as the site of the building. Did they build there. No certainly not as he had already arranged it for himself. I understand. He came first. Yes he came first and he stayed which was quite the natural thing for him to do.

The forty-fourth one married again. No one meant to come to the wedding absolutely no one and he said I am marrying and they said who is it to be and he said I know what you believe and they said how can you believe that you are to be married again. What is the marriage ceremony that you refer to. I refer to the marriage ceremony. Is that so.

The forty-fifth, all the immediate present and those immediately present, all those present will please answer that they are present now. And what do they all say. All those who are present say so. We were very nearly pioneers in this movement. And why are you so frequently referred to, because when they refer to me they mean me.

The forty-sixth prominent man is the one who connected them to their country. My country all the same they have their place there. And why do you tell their names. I tell their names because in this way I know that one and one

and one and one and one and one and one and one and one
and one and one and one and one and one and one and one
and one and one and one and one and one and one and one
make a hundred. It is very difficult to count in a foreign
language.

The forty-seventh does do what he expected to do. He
expected to have what he has include what he was to have
and it did and then when he went again he went again and
again. After that all the same he said all the same I am very
well satisfied.

The forty-eighth placed them there. Where did he place
them. Exactly what do you mean by placing them, he was
asked and he answered. I placed them and they were
equally distant from the different places that were near
them. Is this the way you choose a capital they said. Yes
indeed he said, that is as you may say the result of the
influence of Spanish. Oh yes they replied not entirely
understanding but really he was right. He was undoubtedly
in the right.

The forty-ninth, what habits had this one formed, you may
say that he can be mentioned as being the one who was
bestowed again and again on elephants and mosses. It is
queer that fountains have mosses and forests elephants.
And why is it astonishing that we have heard him when he
was mentioning that he went there, we do not know. Show
me he said and they opened their eyes. Why do you stare,
and why did they. We do not care. Yes do please me. We
please ourselves.

The fiftieth, why did you expect me. We expected you because you had announced yourself and you are usually
punctual. How did you learn to be punctual. Because we
have had the habit of waiting for the rain. Does that make
one punctual. It does. This is what has been bought. Buying

is a vindication of roads. But and stay, stay and buy. By and by. Yes Sir.

The fifty-first one has to say what do you command. What is sweating, that is what I like says Mike, the fifty-first one has an understanding of resisting. He had it said of him that he could countenance alarmingly the destruction of a condition. Why are conditions connected with what I have not said. I said the account, was there an account of it on account of it.

The fifty-second has as an established fact the fact that the account given is the one that makes him furnish everything. Did he furnish it all and was it wise to apprise him that there were many who had religiously speaking an interest in interpretation. This sounds like nonsense. What do you mean by spiritual, what do you. Mike said what do you mean by spiritual what do you. They wished to say that they did not wish anything tried again and again. Be rested. You be rested.

The fifty-third have you heard that fifty and fifty are evenly divided. Have you heard about the way they say it. All of them come again and say it. We say it and they say it. May we say it. I have not forgotten that the fifty-third prominent man is the one that has the most anxious air.

The fifty-fourth one is the one that has been left to study industrialism. No one asks is there merit in that. No one says that there is something noble in that. No one says how do you study a subject. No one idolises Frank. Don't they indeed.

The fifty-fifth is very pretty in any language. How do you do is one way of looking at it. He minds it the most and the shape of it very much. He is very easily offended and he believes in a reference. I refer to you and to you and to you. I always refer to you. I refer to you and I refer you to him and I refer her to them and they refer them to me. Can you see why. Do you understand why they have no need to go and come, to sit down to get up and to walk around.

The fifty-sixth measures what he has done by what he will do. He measures it all and means to react. Action and reaction are equal and possible and we relieve the strain. In this way we arrange for hope and pleasure. This is what we say unites us all to-day.

The fifty-seventh is admirably speaking radiant when he has no annoyances. And why does he continue to know that a lieutenant colonel is in command. Why does he know it. Dear me why does he know it.

The fifty-eighth one is alright. How do the hours come to be longer. Longer than what, longer than English french, Italian, North and South American Japanese and Chinese.

The fifty-ninth marries when he marries, and he is married to me. Do not fail to see him and hear him and rehearse with him and molest him. He has an organic wit.

The sixtieth is actually rested. He has come to be reasonably industrious. He had and he has come to be reasonably industrious. In this way he is successful.

The lieutenant colonel was found dead with a bullet in the back of his head and his handkerchief in his hand.

The sixty-first one has had a very astonishing career. He said that he would never mention another and he never did, he also foresaw the re-establishment of every crisis and he went ahead he went in and out and he foresaw that youth is not young and that the older ones will not seem older and then he imagined expresses. In this way he established his success. I have not mentioned his name.

The sixty-second was just the same. He entered and he came and he came away and no one cared to share expenses.

No one cared to share expenses. What did you say. No one cared to share expenses. He was privileged to increase paler nights and he always measured investigation. How can you investigate privileges. By not curtailing expenses. Thank you for all your thoughts. Give your best thoughts. Thank you for all your thoughts.

The sixty-third, we all have heard of regiments called the sixty-third. Reform regiments in time and they have magnificent beginnings. Do not reform them in time and they progress fairly. Do not reform them at all and they will not necessarily decrease. I say the sixty-third one is the one who came to be celebrated because of this. Because of this he came to be the one that one of the ones that are mentioned in this list.

The sixty-fourth we are a nation of sixty-fourth. Do you remember how a great many of them sat together. Do you and do you remember what they said. My impression was that they had not spoken. My impression was that they had not spoken then. Never again. It is hard to love your father-in-law. Hard almost impossible.

The sixty-fifth, there is a standard for the sixty-fifth. This is his standard. He comes to it and he is very well indeed. Is he. Yes he is very well indeed.

The sixty-sixth, how are you when you are steady. He steadily repeats himself. Do you mean he allows you to feel that he does so. He does indeed.

The sixty-seventh has this advantage. It is an advantage that is easily enjoyed.

The sixty-eighth all small culmination meets with this as their reward. We reward when and where we reward and we reward with rewards. And this is the use of a guardian, where it is guarded it is as well guarded as ever.

The sixty-ninth how authoritative he is and he was. He

was able to arrange for everything again and again and he said with hesitation why do I like to make sweets. Sweets to the sweet said some one.

The seventieth come again and listen were the origin and the beginning of his success. Come again and do not go away. Come again and stay and in this way he succeeded. He was successful. Have you meant to go away he would say. Oh no indeed he meant to stay they would say. And he meant to stay. He was successful in his heyday and he continued to be successful and he is succeeding to-day. When you say how can you feel as you feel we say, that is the way to succeed. That is just the way to succeed. He says I have succeeded.

The seventieth do I remember whether I do or I don't. I think I usually do that is to say I always have. Does that mean you always will. I think so. I gather from what I saw at the door that you wanted me to come in before.

The seventy-first believe me at first. At first we believed that that was because they were so many that had been equal to this one. And then we accompanied them. They were not regularly identified. Nor was he, why did he and because, why did he, because he did double the pansies. You understand that this is symbolical. No one has really more than doubled the pansies.

The seventy-second for in this way there is a second the seventy-second managed to see me. And where were they all. They were all in there. And why did no one declare themselves faultless. This was very nearly a dish, a nest of dishes. Do you remember that play. A nest of dishes. This and the painting of a garden scene made an astonishing measure for measure. Answer blindly to this assurance and be assured that all the pleasure is yours.

The seventy-third has nearly spoken. He said I see rapidly

I compose carefully, I follow securely and I arrange dexterously, I predict this for me.

The seventy-fourth how often have both had children. I said that he should not change he should continue with girls. I said she should not change she should continue with girls. She changed and he did not. He continued with girls.

The seventy-fifth very many actually count. They count one two three four five six seven.

The seventy-sixth one is the one that has not often met nor often been met nor very often met them yet. They are there they do declare that they are there. And why publish data.

The seventy-seventh really places it. He places there with a great deal of care. And when he was twelve he sang in public. There are a great many reasons for it. This is one of them. The reason I have given is their reason. Do be satisfied with their reason. Do not be worried do not be worried at all nor do not be at all worried. Be satisfied. Be very well satisfied.

The seventy-eighth do you remember about him do you really explain when you explain that he loved lacing and unlacing and releasing and separate silence. Do you really credit this with that. Do you do so fairly.

The seventy-ninth was originally delicious, delicious as delicious as the excellent repast which was offered. Do you remember how she wrote offer, offered. Do you and do you prefer exchange that is barter to pleasure in reason. I believe in pleasure and the reason the reason for it.

The eightieth how do you manage to mention a number separately. It is a specialty a specialty of wine. That is very fine in you and it all proves to me that I have faith and a future.

The eighty-first at first the eighty-first was the one who

had made the fruit house who had the fruit house made there where it was very singular that he could understand that there was land.

You see it is like this land is made to be near by so that one can see it. Land is made to be understood to be there. So there was naturally no distribution of land and land. Do you understand, Lizzie do you understand. These were naturally there here there and everywhere. We have principally met whether we need to or not. I do complain of sitting there. Not here. No not here.

The eighty-second, was it we say was it by means of a hammer or by means of a rock, was it by hammer or by rock that we felt that the future was one with the present. Do you know by what means rockets signal pleasure pain and noise and union, do you know by what means a rock is freed when it is not held too tightly held in the hand. Many hold what they hold and he held what was best to settle in Seattle. Why do you care for climate. Why do you. I know.

The eighty-third, tell me about him. I will. He was never neglected nor was he especially willing to sing, a great many ceased to secure singing. You mean they found Saturday intolerable. That is just it that is just what I wish to say, you put it in that way and certainly very certainly a great many kind of birthdays are taken for granted. Granted.

The eighty-fourth that too might be taken to be the same as if it were one number the more and yet if you think delicately and you do think so you will see why I say no it is not the same. Now supposing he were famous would he understand it as you say he does understand fame. Would he. Oh you question me so narrowly and I might say I didn't mean and then what would you say. I would say I just want to be praised. There that is permanent.

157

The eighty-fifth is the one did I mention that this too might be the number of a regiment. You see they say that there are more there you mean as to one thousand and four thousand, there are more there.

He has given as the reason that he knows the difference between Christmas New Year Easter and Thanksgiving. He has given this as a reason.

The eighty-sixth is the one to measure by animals. A dog another dog and a woman two lions and a man a central surface a lion a dog and a man and two men and more introduction. I introduce you to him and to him. Do you introduce him too often. I do not think so. No I do not think so.

The eighty-seventh study the eighty-seventh one carefully and tell me what it is that you notice. I notice that in different positions one sees a different distinction. You mean you always distinguish him. Oh so readily. And when you smile does he smile at all, he smiles very readily when you smile at all. And does he furnish you with agreeable merriment. Very agreeably so. Tell him so it will please him. I do. I will.

The eighty-eighth furnish the eighty-eighth with the means of furnishing. We furnish everything. He furnishes everything. In this way we cannot mean what has been made clear. We cannot mean that he plans this.

The eighty-ninth remember that when you remember the eighty-ninth it was not so happily bowed to as it might have been if all pages were printed as they came. We like printing it all the same. Now just what do you mean by that. I mean that very rapidly he refreshes himself.

The eighty-ninth, forty made the eighty-ninth clearly the half of that number. There are a number of them aren't they and each one every one more than one, one and one, they all stay over there. If for instance there had been one continuation where then would they place the succession. Where would they. You don't ask where did they. You don't really ask me anything.

The ninetieth is the ninetieth one to-day. To-day come to care to stay. How do you. Dear me how can you use it as if it was a cane. How can you. Please how can you. I can do all this and all the time have you discovered anything. She did, keys and a kitchen. Not a mistake. It was not a mistake.

The ninety-first who knows about this one, it is not easy to plan for it, eat for it or trouble for it. It is not easy to manage to say to-day and yesterday and very likely every other day. It is not easy. I say it isn't easy.

The ninety-second and does he attend to all of it. Do you attend to all of it. I am not easily convinced that they attend to all of it. Do they attend to all of it. All that I know about it is that whether they do or whether they do not we have a system of triple mirrors. In this way we see where they come. Where do they come from. I see abundance geographically.

The ninety-third, every one has heard of the ninety-third. Naturally, and now what do you mean by rushing. What do you mean by rushing in here and saying am I in it. What do you mean by doing that. Even if you were in it you would not be heard from so definitely. Be reasonable, leave it all to me. When this you see remember that you are to wait for me. I can say this very quickly.

The ninety-fourth marries he marries them, now how can you know whether in saying this I mean what you mean does this bother you at all does it annoy you, can you be obstinate in asserting that we have the same meaning that you mean and that I mean that he marries them. Think about this carefully and when you are thoroughly prepared to be generous give me your answer. I answer for him.

The ninety-fifth, remember the ninety-fifth. Ninety-nine is ninety-nine, and the ninety-fifth has a very good evening. Good evening. It is not our custom to say good evening.

The ninety-sixth and more and more. You were given to reconciling floods with fire. This is a noisy day. May I look again.

The ninety-seventh hears me has heard me when I have said do not care to hear Cornelius Vanderbilt. The ninety-seventh is excellent in his way, he is very excellent in that way and does prepare his share. Do you prepare your share. And do you estimate your share correctly. Have you ever mistaken anything and put it away there with your share. No neither of you have, neither of you have ever done so.

The ninety-eighth, the ninety-eighth and the ninety-ninth, the ninety-eighth is the one we see when we look. We look and we look. How do we look. We look very pretty. Do we look well. We look very well.

The ninety-ninth who is the ninety-ninth, as for me I prefer to call tissue paper silk paper. Do you prefer to do so by the year. Tissue paper is a thin paper, and silk paper is a thin paper. One might say that tissue paper is a paper made of thin tissue. It is sometimes called silk paper. It is made of the same material but is not quite so thin.

The Hundredth. When you believe me you believe me very often don't you. I believe that Andrew D. White and many worked all day and I believe that Andrew D. White and many others worked all night I believe that many others worked all day and that many others worked all night. I believe that many others are so had I not better say are often an addition. Then can you say that you do like to see. Yes

I do like to see you here. And then why do you follow me.
You follow me. I follow you follow you follow me. You do
follow me.
One hundred and won. When this is done will you make
me another one.

20

American Biography And Why Waste It

Do you see any connection between yes and yesterday, I will repeat this, do you see any connection between yes and yesterday.

There is a way of recording an arbitrary collision but in inventing barbed wire and in inventing puzzles there is no arbitrary collision. Not at all.

They murmured about excess not about excess not about exceeding their limit. They murmured about success. Be brief.

I found a way of saying arrange for many more. And then they went away.

Second to none and have you been interfered with, I ask you again have you ever been interfered with either in there or where. Where have you been interfered with and where have you been when you have been interfered with there.

Now understand.

In the future, in the past because there has been really a previous occasion, in the future and then why does it matter. Why does it matter particularly.

Now tell us about their principles. The principal thing is that contracts why do contracts come along. Why do they. Why do they include all brushes. All brushes are alright.

When you have seen the result of reflection reflection does result in this when you have seen the result of reflection reflection does result in this.

And narrowly in cream.

Satisfy the spectacle.

I satisfy all the places. In place of this place me.

Once more we come to inventions.

Did he say he wished me to relieve rolls.

What was it he said about reminding. I never remind them.

Can you think and listen can you think and listen can you think and listen.

Can you think of them and listen to me.

This is why we stay in their way.

What did the first one say. They say they are endowed with memory circumstance occasion and reconstruction. Can you call it reconstruction to add, to begin or to acquit. Can you.

He smiled and I smiled. Then there is coercion, cohesion and administration, then there are authentic dispatches, then there is recognition. I recognise him, he recognises me, they recognise us, and when we hear them say what are your branches, I wonder if they mean stems.

The introducers are highly educated.

Not wishing to begin.

One little Indian two little Indian three little Indian boys, four little five little six little seven little eight little Indian boys. To an American an Indian means a red skin not an inhabitant of the east or west Indies or of India.

When we are astounded astonished concerned received or intimidated we do not recount roses.

Roses grow and rhododendrons and woods and woods, the poor man's overcoat.

Woods the poor man's overcoat and I'll say so.

Now then begin again, begin with Adam the Adams and then pour easily pour out. Do you easily pour out. Do you easily pour out about their cold, this was told. This was what they hold to be the return of the collection.

Let me see.

To begin with what did he say. What did he say.

To begin with what they remember.

They remembered that very much and they were nickled and embroidered. To be nickeled, how do you reveal how do you dare to presume everything.

Goodness knows.

I can feel that.

They were met by themselves, and suggestions, how easily they parody suggestions, how easily they parry suggestions.

Cover me they care for me. They care, they do care.

They and they do care.

I do not freely recollect speaking.

When they were there when they were in there he said he he said of them he did not say this to them, he said to them come and be able to remember everything. He remembers why they fasten trees to trees. In our country they do not fasten trees to trees.

What do you do. We commence to supplant, we supplant fruit and oranges, and how often do you prune, a great many make verbs. This will surprise you.

This will surprise you.

I remember that some one said that one should arrange for a longer term, twenty-five years roll around so quickly. Now what is the difference between age and ages.

What is the difference and why do you marry.

What do you exchange for directions. He directs me to come and to go. He directs me to go and to come.

Did you hear what she said, they are going to have summer time in April in New York city and Chicago.

You were pleased not to hear them. I was very pleased not to hear them.

I did not hear them at all.

And now I wish to tell exactly how I have been impressed, I have been very well impressed. For instance memory and then discussion, analysis and then barter, and did you feel that when they went further they adventured. To me it really does not seem so. And to them it does not seem so. They were not at all elevated to this degree.

They said that they would say so and they said nothing at all about it they did not carry this there in their favour. Indeed one might say that they were blameless. They were more readily not altered. An altar is made by the rest of their stay. All stay. They stay anyway.

And now to attribute. I attribute this to this. To what do you attribute this.

There is no flattery in this.

Do you remember how often we had cake. Do you remember how often we had butter. Do you remember how often we had what we needed. Do you remember how often we thought about it and how often a great many people circled.

We know about blame and circles and now we know about considerably added currents. The currents that come come there. Where. Where did you say.

Call me louder.

Do you remember how you affected her. And when did you state this.

When did you state this.

And now be able to state what I find to relate.

Distributed.

We can praise that verb. We distribute all of the same letters to make the letters. A great many say what letters.

Do a great many say what letters.

It is a reminder. Call it a reminder. Let me glory in messages. Let me.

Now then they do not press hurriedly. And this is not assertion. Not at all. Not at all. Not that at all.

He arouses him.

Not that way.

He arouses the land you mean that he does not only use that he does not abuse. Do I mean religion, do I mean men women and their children. Do I mean that there is a third. Do you mean what you have heard. Do you mean. What do you mean.

And now then as to appetite. We have a very good appetite. Almost any one can think faster than another man can talk, I wonder if that was so yesterday.

I gently feel. You do not mean that you feel gentle, I gently feel of it. That before this.

And now we know we are rescinded.

The cannon of Australia makes a noise and we say and they say we are telling how we found our country to be the land of liberty of which we sing. The cannon of the Indian makes that noise and they do not say that they know the difference between that and everything. Everything else is opposed to that. I see why they do not like noise and make a noise. I know. The reason is this when they went they were still and still when they were there they were there, where there, and they knew they heard that, they hear that they hear that, they do not hear that they have come there, this they do not hear there, they do not listen to hear, nor do they hear by ear, listen and you do not hear, but they they were there and they met to declare, what, the air, to the air and by the air. Here here is not there. Everywhere is not there nor is it here nor there. I declare and they declare. And the air. We do not recognise an heir.

So there.

Responsibilities are all there, and they are not to be followed by prayer there, they are to be followed by the songs as sung. Responsibilities are not to be followed there, they ought not to be followed there by prayer but they ought to be followed by the songs as sung, they ought not to be flung there they ought not to be followed by prayer there. I know the result I know that result. A responsibility followed by another is plenty good enough.

I do not think that all of this is very unpleasant and not very affable. Do you not feel that way about it. I do come to think of it. I do come to think of it and there are three men and one man. We know that together three men and one man make four men. We know this of them and knowing this we can mean that there is one man and that there are three men and together the three men and the one man together there are four men and when they say we have a remarkable opportunity they mean by this an imagination just as has the president.

He knows everything but the third, third what, but the third congratulation. Do not mention it by yesterday. Do not measure by chairs. You know how they sign. They sign by chairs. And how are hours changed. Hours are changed by settling this and they say we knew when we came. And they say the same. In this way we weigh the same. Do you remember me for this. I do not want to be persistent. I do not want to have the blame. We can claim that we do nothing for fame.

We can claim we do claim we shall claim shall you claim what we claim. No. I told you so.

Now then to liberate adequate.

A responsibility will be followed by another.

Thank you.

Recall, do you recall this at all. They made and they made it they made it all, they made it and they made it for them and they made all of it for them they made all that was made.

What was it that was said. How does he say it. Who are you to say how does he say it and why and why does he say it, because he had it. No one caresses you. Do you hear. No one caresses you.

Now to finance lumps.

We do not know about clouds and lumps. We do not know where to go. He said I will tell you this to move you.

And now not the same.

I said I would not measure for them, I would not measure more than that for them. I said I would not measure more for them than that.

Soldiers. How do you mean soldiers.

Come to think of pillows. He does not know the meaning of harassed and yet they are all there.

They said, we do not see that this is of any use. He said, I came and I was born there. And they said, we are born to surprise. And he said. Do they surprise beside. And they all say that they have all preserved their cinches. Now listen to this. Inches. Now again, all are not elbowed again.

We say they are not heavier than they say.

Not heavier than that, they say.

In Spain there is no rain.

When this you see remember me.

There is no rain in Spain.

When this you see remember me.

Do not repeat this as formerly.

In learning in learning to feed, we feed the same number and with what, I ask you and with what.

We feed the same number and we feed them here.

I have endangered no one more than that. They have endangered no one more than that. And they have said it successively and do they frolic about.

Words do.

Do they frolic about.

What do they frolic about.

This brings me to another collision. I feel you are sincere.

How many heads are there ahead.

How many are there ahead.

How many are there at the head.

I would like a photograph of that said Captain Dyer.

What he saw of them made him see that.

Now then tell me why can you at your discretion tell them that you can tell them apart.

Now what do you mean by this.

I can deliver crowns, you mean those that kings wore. We never mention that as rain. I can deliver them from there. I can deliver these from them. You are not here again and again. Nor for mounting.

Recall having sent articles.

I know exactly how to receive their weight.

Do you read.

Thank all who thank me.

Other races.

I do and you do too you do conceal clouds. Clouds shine and you shine. All of it, do, do all of it. Do do all of it.

There is not going to be much more of that.

A biography.

Eugene George Herald was refused because of his accentuation. We do not accentuate, we increase in regard to measure sound and sections. In this way we are united to stand.

169

21

Lend a Hand or Four Religions

Look up and not down look right and not left look forward and not back and lend a hand.
We lend you lend they lend he lends they lend you lend we
lend he lends.
And then they tell to-day they tell it to-day they tell it
to-day and yesterday and to-morrow.

First religion	My sister
Second religion	My sister and her sister
Third religion	My sister or my sister
Fourth religion	Your sister.

First religion advances and then sees some one she advances
and then she sees some one.
Second religion   Second religion they advance
and they see some one, they advance and they see some
one as they advance.
Third religion   She advances and she sees some
one, she sees some one or she advances.
Fourth religion   As she advances she sees some
one. Some one is seen by her as she advances.
Fourth religion   As she advances.
Fourth religion   As she advances she is led.
Third religion   As she advances or as she ad-
vances or is she led.
Second religion   As they advance they are led.
First religion   Is she led.
First religion   As she advances is she led.

First religion   Is she led as she advances.
That is the name of a house isn't it.
And a well.
First religion as she advances. Furnish a house as well.
Second religion as they advance. They furnish a house as well.
Third religion as she has advanced. Has she furnished a house as well or has she furnished a house as well as she has furnished a house.
Fourth religion as she is advancing and she will furnish a house as well.
Fourth religion   Very well to advance to see some one then and to furnish a house as well.
Third religion, third religion to advance and to see some one or to furnish a house as well or to advance and furnish a house as well or to see some one or furnish a house as well.
Second religion   They advance and as they advance they see some one and they furnish a house as well. As well furnish a house. They might furnish a house as well.
First religion   She might furnish a house as well she might see some one and furnish a house as well, she might advance and she might see some one as she advanced and she might furnish a house as well.
First religion   First religion attaches it first religion attaches it.
Second religion   They attach it, they attach it to that and which ever water, kneeling, in a kneeling posture.
Third religion   She attaches it or in that way kneeling in a way in that way, in that way kneeling and being a chinese Christian meditatively. And there where there is water flowing there where she attaches it she attaches to it or she attaches it to it there where the water

171

is flowing or kneeling there or beside it in a way of kneeling.
Fourth religion   Does fatigue make a sensitive alliance and reliance. She attaches it and as she attaches she is kneeling there and she is kneeling there where she is kneeling in a box there where the water is flowing there where she attaches it there. Where she attaches there where she is where she is as she is kneeling there in a box and the water is flowing there beside the water where it is flowing there she attaches it there.
Fourth religion   I am not losing it too.
Third religion   I am not losing it too or I am not losing it too or I am not losing it.
Second religion   They are not losing it they are not losing it too. They are not and they are not losing it too.
First religion   She is not losing it too.
First religion   They will furnish a house as well. As she advances she sees some one and she kneeling in a box beside the water where it is flowing and she will furnish a house as well is she losing as being kneeling beside the water where it is flowing in being a christian will she furnish a house as well. In losing it as she is advancing and she sees some one as she is advancing will she furnish a house as well.
Second religion   Will they furnish a house as well. In being kneeling beside the water where it is flowing will they furnish a house as well. In advancing and seeing some one as they are advancing and in kneeling beside the water where the water is flowing will they love will they love it they are kneeling beside the water where it is flowing and will they furnish a house as well.
Third religion   Will she furnish a house as well or will she be kneeling beside the water where the water is

flowing or will she be advancing and as she is advancing will she see some one or will she furnish a house as well. Will she furnish a house as well or will she be furnishing a house as well.

Fourth religion   Will she be kneeling beside the water where the water is flowing and will she be losing it and will she furnish a house as well and will she see some one as she is advancing and will she be a christian and will she furnish a house as well. Will she be kneeling beside the water. Will she advance and will she furnish the house as well. Will she be kneeling there where the water is flowing. She attaches to it this, she attaches to it.

Fourth religion   The sky is blue.

The hills are green.

She is green too.

And her eyes are blue.

She attaches something. As she advances she sees some one. She kneels beside the water there where the water is flowing. She is a chinese christian. She is losing it. Does she furnish a house as well.

Fourth religion   Does she furnish a house as well.

Fourth religion   Are grasses grown and does she observe that the others remove them. Are grasses grown four times yearly. Does she see the grasses that are grown four times yearly. Does she very nearly remove them. Does she remove them and do they very nearly grow four times yearly. Does she as she sees some one does she advance and does she very nearly remove the green grasses that grow nearly four times yearly. In this country they do.

Third religion   Does she very nearly or does she see the green grasses grow four times yearly. Does she remove them or does she know that they do grow four times yearly. Does she see some one as she advances or does she kneel there where the water is flowing or does she furnish a house as well. Does she nearly remove them.

Second religion   Do they see the grasses grow four times yearly and do they remove them and do they advance and see some one and do they touch it and do they lose it and do they see them grow almost four times yearly nearly four times nearly.

First religion   Does she almost see the grasses grow four times yearly does she see the green grasses grow four times yearly and is she nearly kneeling beside the water where the water is flowing. Does she touch it and does she remove it and does she see the green grasses grow nearly four times yearly. Does she see some one as she advances and does she kneel by the water is she kneeling by the water where the water is flowing. I do not think so. She is feeling that the green grasses grow nearly four times yearly.

First religion   She is feeling that the grasses grow four times yearly and does she furnish a house as well. Let her think of a stable man and a stable can be a place where they care for the Italians every day. And a mission of kneeling there where the water is flowing kneeling, a chinese christian, and let her think of a stable man and wandering and a repetition of counting. Count to ten. He did. He did not. Count to ten. And did she gather the food as well. Did she gather the food as well. Did she separate the green grasses from one another. They grow four times yearly. Did she see some one as she was advancing and did she remove what she had and did she lose what she touched and did she touch it and the water there where she was kneeling where it was flowing. And are stables a place where they care for them as well.

Second religion   Did they think of stables as well and did they see the grasses grow four times yearly and did

174

they kneel by the water where the water was flowing and did they as they advanced did they see some one and did they touch it and did they lose it and did they furnish a house as well.

Third religion   Did she think a stable was for a stableman or for the caring for Italians or did she see some one as she was advancing or did she kneel beside the water where the water was flowing or did she see grasses grow four times yearly.

Fourth religion   Did she see the stables and did she know that stables are used to take care of Italians and did she know that green grasses grow four times yearly and did she kneel by the water there where the water was flowing and did she kneel there a chinese christian and did she see some one as she advanced and did she touch it and did she lose it and did she furnish a house as well.

Fourth religion   Did he count, count ten. If you count count ten, do you count with your lips moving. If she counts, counts ten does she count with her lips moving. If she kneels and if she kneels does she kneel by the water there where the water is flowing and does she see the green grasses grow four times yearly. Does she count ten and does she count ten with her lips moving. And does she as she advances does she see some one and does she know that a stable is a place to care for Italians. And does she count ten and as she counts ten are her lips moving.

Third religion   As she counts ten or as she counts ten, as she counts ten are her lips moving. If she counts ten does she count ten and are her lips moving. Are her lips moving as she counts ten. On Thursday actors and actresses are arriving. As she counts ten are her lips moving or is it Thursday and are actors and actresses arriving.

Second religion   As they count ten are their lips moving. Do they as they count do they have to have their lips moving. On Thursday do they have to have actors and actresses arriving and do they nearly see green grass growing four times yearly and do they kneel there where the water is flowing. As they count are their lips moving, do they count ten and when they count do their lips move are there lips moving.

First religion   On Thursday when Thursday comes and actors and actresses are coming when she counts ten does she move her lips while she is counting. When she is moving her lips is she counting and does she count ten and does she very nearly kneel there where the water is flowing and does she furnish a house as well and as she advances does she see some one and does she nearly see the green grass growing four times yearly and does she know that a stable is a place where Italians are taken care of and does she choose and refuse and lose and does she nearly see her lips moving as she counts ten and does she nearly believe that she can clearly count to ten. Does she count to ten when her lips are moving. Does she know that a stable is to take care of Italians and does she furnish a house as well.

Very well.

First religion   Not even hardly. When there was a settled plan and sleep.

She sleeps, she keeps, she keeps she sleeps.

Not even hardly.

I plan to satisfy their blessing.

In this way she can say that they were not in her way, in her way she does say that they are not in her way in their way she can say they were there in their way. Explain it to me.

176

They understood everything.

She needed that and this and in there. Did she say that they were expected to-day.

Second religion   Did they say that they had expected to stay that they had expected to come to-day.

Third religion   Did she or did she not stay. Did she say that they were expected to-day or did she say that she keeps them there or are they coming to stay. Or are they coming to stay.

Fourth religion   She keeps them and they share what they have with what they have. She stays there and did she say that she had been in the way. It sweetens volume to stay. Do you understand how they feel how Italians feel how chinese Christians a stableman, grasses, houses and water actors and actresses and men who are men then how how do they feel when they see separate volumes. Separate volumes.

Fourth religion   I pass I surpass she passes she surpasses, she passes and passes and she surpasses the folded roses. They fold roses and she surpasses them. She surpasses them in this way. And this is the way to fold roses. She says this is their way of folding. And she does kneel there. Where. Where does she kneel. Where did she kneel. When did she kneel and why did she pass and surpass pass and surpass them.

Second religion   Mix it, in mixing them you can always say one three four two. In mixing them and surpassing them they can always say one three four two one three four two one three four two. And can they fold their roses too.

Third religion   If she folded roses or if she folded roses for them, if she folded roses for them did she pass them or did she pass them and fold roses for them or did she surpass them in folding roses for them. Did she or did she not surpass them.

First religion   Melons melons what did she say choosing melons is the difficulty. And did she pass them, did she surpass did she surpass them in this way. Do not choose them in this way, choose them and use them choose them and stay and put folded roses away in this way.

First religion   Did they gather their excellent father. Did they gather their excellent mother. Did they gather. Did they gather that their excellent mother did they gather that their excellent father, did they gather. Did she gather. Did she gather that she did gather and did she gather this from them, did she gather this from her did she gather this. Who says this. Who said that. Did she gather that.

Second religion   Did they gather that their excellent father went to the winning of their excellent mother and to the winning of one another and to widening of every other one. Did they gather that they saw that in this way there where there was a plan to succeed when and where there was sawing. We hear it.

Third religion   Did she or did they, did they or did she gather that their excellent that their excellent mother were father and mother or did she hear that the sawing was there where they were sent unaware. They were sent there or were they sent there. Were they sent where they went and did they go or did they go where the sawing was meant to be done without sun. We know that the sawing is done in the sun or without the sun when the sun has been seen or has been seen.

Fourth religion   And did she know and did she

go and did she know that they gather that they can gather an excellent father and an excellent mother and she needs to know that the fourth also says so.

Fourth religion   Merely whether it is their celebration that makes their pleasure so prepared. She is prepared. When is she prepared. She prepared them for this. The fourth says so, and we say it is the third.

The third religion   If the third, we criticise the third, if the third and the third is prepared or if she is prepared and the celebration is prepared. If the third is prepared or if the celebration is prepared, to please her.

Second religion   If they are prepared, have they shared the preparation of their celebration. Glasses share, they prepare to keep an orange tree protected out there. Not glasses nor glass. Nor glass nor glasses. She passes in and out and she leaves no roses about.

First religion   We prepared what she had to say. I was not indifferent, nor was she indifferent nor was she more indifferent. We must state this to be here. She prepares the celebration, she prepares the celebration. She prepares the glass to protect the orange trees as they pass. The orange trees pass. The orange trees do not pass us.

First religion   First religion can be added. First religion the first religion can be added it can be added to the one and that one and it can be added.

Second religion   The second religion can be added. They can be added. In this instance they can be added.

Third religion   The third religion or is it added to the third religion or is the third religion. If the third religion is added then she adds it. She has added it.

Fourth religion   She is adding to the fourth

religion. She is adding to the fourth religion. She is adding this and to the fourth religion. The fourth religion is added to this.

The fourth Religion.

Fourth religion   Meadows for men and more meadows then. We know how they lie and where they lie. The meadows lie in between.

Third religion   Meadows are seen to lie in between and she or what was it in case it was there. Four of them, there were three of them. In three of them there was one in each of the three of them.

Second religion   Does she remember the scene and there with the glare of the sun shut out there is no need indeed there is no need we know how the sides are made. They are made indeed they are made.

First religion   By no means by their means by her means she saw seven of them lean. They lean as if they were inclosed and we refused them. Not ardently. Remember that the meadows are there.

First religion   First for a religion. At first for a religion. They were for a religion. She was the first for the religion.

First religion   At first she had always thought she had always fought for the religion and she was kneeling there where the water was flowing and she was a chinese christian and she could furnish a house as well and the meadows were for men and the orange trees pass and are inclosed with glass.

Second religion   They were second to religion they were to second and they were to second all the second religion was the same as the first. They were kneeling there where the water was flowing and they were seeing green grasses growing four times yearly and they can gather an excellent father and an excellent mother and they surpass and they pass.

Third religion   The third of the third or the. third, the third was at first the third and then the third was there or was she kneeling there where the water was flowing and did she furnish a house as well. Indeed as well.

Fourth religion   Did she furnish a house as well as a fourth religion as a fourth religion as a fourth religion did she know that stables are made and stablemen to take care of Italians and did she know that meadows are made for men and did she know and did she say so did she know the fourth religion.

Fourth religion   The shepherds spend the summer in the mountains and the winter in the plains in this way they and the sheep are cool in summer and warm in winter and what do their families do. They do not always accompany them. She was the one who said how do you do, I forgive you everything and there is nothing to forgive. She was the one who said, how do you do I forgive you everything and there is nothing to forgive.

Third religion   They carried their happiness there and they meant to meet with the shepherds and their sheep. How do you bleat. Shepherds have animals too. They advance before the sheep and they carry the baskets and in this way they act as leaders. Who can lead them.

Second religion   Question the question is who can prefer them. Can they use a drum can they use a fair can they use a road and can they use it or have they measured or have they forgotten that they or they or they that they can convince them.

First religion   She saw me and she said two will stay and two will go away, two will go away and two will stay and two will stay and two will go away. Can you go away so soon.

First religion   First religion here.

Second religion   Second religion here.

Third religion   Third religion here.

Fourth religion   Fourth religion here.

Fourth religion   Fourth religion being here and having her and she having been and she is perfection.

Third religion   Third religion being here or is she perfection third religion is here and she is perfection. Third religion or is she perfection.

Second religion   Second religion and they are here and they are perfection and they are here and perfection.

First religion   She is here and perfection.

First religion   In the way in her way in her way in that way in that way in my way in my way in her way in her way in our way in our way in her way she can say and she can say, she can say I spend it and intend it. She can say that sheep give way when they do not stray. They do not stray, they do not stray at all.

Second religion   In their way they are there to stay in their way not in their way no not in their way not at all in their way and not at all in the way not at all in the way. They have an intention and we hear it now they have an intention and they hear it now, they have an intention. In the midst in the midst we know what sun is. This is their hope and there are leaves to cover and caress. So there are.

Third religion   In her way who mentions Saturday, or in her way who mentions Monday or in her way who mentions that they are in her way or in her way, away in a way, and in any way she bows to please. Does it please or does it betray that abundance is on the way.

Fourth religion   I mean that she can mean that she can mean to stay. That she can mean to stay.

More religion

Fourth religion   More religion fourth religion. More religion or third religion. More religion and second religion. More religion first religion.

First religion   I feel that here I feel that here they seem to lie and grow and feel and are tall and dark and large and delicate and there they are full and soft and rich and delicate. I feel that here they are full and rich and tall and there they are not small they are large and full and rich and tall and delicate.

I describe. You describe. What do you describe. What do I describe.

Second religion   I feel that the difference is this. There the colour is of a splendour and rich and full and delicate and here it is high and strong and rich and delicate.

Third religion   Here it is delicate and there it is delicate.

Fourth religion   I describe it as different there than it is here. Here it is rich and full and large and delicate there it is full and rich and warm and delicate.

Fourth religion   If she can gather together and then settle whether the land is found how do you find land readily. She did. How do you find land readily.

Third religion   If she can be found and she can gather it together and she can find land readily is it land that is to be found. Land is found and sold by the pound. Land is found and sold by the pound.

Second religion   Or if they can gather it together

and can find it readily is it land that they have found. Where is land. Land is at hand. When they gather it together they can sell it readily.

First religion   If she gathered it altogether and found that the land was entirely gathered together would she be bound to gather it together entirely and would it be land. Would it be that land.

First religion   Very well.

Second religion   Very very well.

Third religion   Very well very well.

Fourth religion   Very well.

Fourth religion   If she had returned if she had returned would she advance and as she advanced would she have seen some one.

Third religion   If she had returned if she had returned and if she had then advanced would she have seen some one as she advanced

Second religion   If they were returned and they then advanced would they see some one as they advanced.

First religion   When she returned and when she advanced would she see some one as she advanced.

First religion   If she is a stone breaker and has a rope attached to a mountain she would not be a wife for Michael. If she had a rope attached to the mountain she would be a stone breaker and would she see some one as she advanced and would the green grass grow four times yearly. If she had a rope attached to the mountain a stone breaker uses her arms from the elbows and it looks mechanical and she furnishes a house as well. She does not use the rope which is attached to the mountain. That is used by those who roll the stones down to her. She does not kneel there where the water is running.

Second religion   If they had been the ones having the rope attached to the mountain they would be the
ones who did stone breaking and they would be kneeling
there where the water is flowing and where the green grasses
grow four times yearly and they would furnish the house
as well.

Third religion   There where the rope is attached
to the mountain or as she was repeating, is she kneeling there
where the water is flowing or as she was saying is there
any grass growing four times yearly or does she furnish a
house as well.

Fourth religion   The rope attached to the
mountain is for the benefit of those who roll the rocks down
the mountain and the umbrella and the mechanical motion
is hers who is breaking the rocks open and she is observing
that the grass is growing nearly four times yearly. She
can establish this very well.

Fourth religion   She would not wonder if this
were not thunder it should not thunder and she would not
wonder. She would not wonder if this were not thunder.
And what would they see if the sheep did not come to be
seen where it was dry and where it was green.

Second religion   They would not wonder if there
was no thunder they would know that if wool is wet it
weighs more than when it is dry.

Third religion   If she needed to amend what
she said if she needed to mend thread if she needed more
than she said she needed, if she needed more than she said
she needed, why does she kneel there where she said she was
kneeling, why does she prepare to prepare what they need
for feeding. In this way this can stay and I can take it
away in this way.

First religion   If she should hear and wonder

would she wonder if she heard and there was thunder. If there was thunder would she wonder. She would.

First religion   Not round all around but orange and brown and smaller than the second the third and the fourth.

Second religion   Not round all around but yellow and redder and not round altogether but larger than the first and not so large as the third and the fourth.

The third   More round all around but not round altogether or rather not round all around and more orange than yellow and larger than the first or than any of the two others.

Fourth religion   Quite round all around not quite round all around not larger than the second and more yellow.

Fourth religion   They have it there and warmer and if at night it is warmer in the day time it is warmer. They have it there it is warmer.

Third religion   They have it there and it is warmer. If it is warmer in the day time and they have it there they have it there and it is warmer.

The second   They have it there. They have it there because it is warmer there.

First religion   They have it there and it is warmer there and it is warmer there in the daytime and it is warmer there. In the night time it is warm there.

First religion   Can you refuse me can you confuse me can you amuse me can you use me. She said can you. Sweet neat complete tender mender defend her joy alloy and then say that.

Second religion   Can you not confuse this while and that. Can you not refuse this length and that. Can you not amuse this height and that. Can you mention sweet neat complete. Tender mender defender, joy alloy and toy, and more of this.

Third religion   If you did refuse or if you did confuse if you did confuse or if you did refuse and if you mentioned neat sweet complete joy toy alloy, tender mender defender, if you did or if you did scatter them why do you not stay.

Fourth religion   If you did not refuse and confuse and use, if you did not mention sweet neat complete tender mender defender, joy alloy if you did not what would you do instead.

Fourth religion   Very nearly a present and I thank you.

Third religion   Very nearly at present.

Third religion   Very nearly for a present and I thank you.

Second religion   Very nearly and a present and I thank you.

They thank me.

First religion   Very nearly a present and I thank you.

First religion   Indirectly and directly directly and indirectly and do oblige do not oblige them to lead, we know that flocks of sheep can go ahead and to be mentioned. In this way roads smile and roads smile every mile and they advance and pray. Pray here. She can suggest there and there.

Second religion   They can suggest there and there. They have been and they have been here and they say flocks can pray and roads can smile and they can stay and smile and pray and they can say that as they advance they see some one.

Third religion   As she advances she sees some

one. She sees here and there. She hears here and she hears there and she can say or does she hesitate in any way that flocks can lead the way and pray and that roads can all that while in that way come to go that way and they may. She can advance and as she advances she can see some one.

Fourth religion   Can she can she betray her care that she can care to lead and she cannot lead and pray because flocks can lead and can pray and they can see the roads in that way and the roads can stay.

Fourth religion   If she did advance and if she did see some one as she advanced and if she said that there were stablemen there do we hear of stables every where. Is there a stable there and are there chinese christians not to stare but to kneel in prayer there where the water is flowing and there where if she were standing and mechanically moving and a rope was tied to a mountain would she know that the flock was leading and that the flock was leading here was leading them to be here and there. Would she come and would she see the flock as well.

Third religion   If she or the flock were seen to be surrounding the road which was not what was to be told. They surrounded the road. Indeed she can believe it to be she can believe it to be surrounded there.

Second religion   They were mentioned as fairly small and they were mentioned as fairly small. And they were there where they knew that they stood and could they see that they were there and that was the day when they were there and they could they furnish the house as well when they were well and they were very well.

First religion   First religion who knows how to say what can be said when questions are asked and flocks have lead and flocks have lead and ropes have been tied and roads have been wide and been surrounded beside. Thank you.

First religion   I thank you.
Second religion   We thank you.
Third religion   I can thank you.
Fourth religion   I do thank you.
Fourth religion   Thank you.
Fourth religion   She can believe and receive and believe she can receive and she goes where she goes and do they believe and receive they believe and receive they receive and they go where they go.
Third religion   Does she believe does she receive does she go, do they go does she go do they receive does she receive does she believe do they believe do they believe and receive.
Second religion   Do they believe and receive and do they go. Do they go and do they believe and do they receive.
First religion   Does she go.
First religion   No and not yes.
Second religion   Yes and not no.
Third religion   Yes and not no and no and not yes.
Fourth religion   No and not yes.
Fourth religion   No and not no and not yes.
Fourth religion   The fourth religion is the religion of which we have spoken.
Third religion   The third religion is the religion of which we have spoken.
The second religion   Is that religion is it the religion of which we have spoken.
The first religion   Is it the religion of which we have spoken.

First religion	She has spoken.
Second religion	They have spoken.
Third religion	She spoke.
Fourth religion	She has spoken.
Fourth religion	I can see the sea.
Third religion	I can see that sea.
Second religion	I can see to the sea.
First religion	I see the sea.
First religion	And she should see to it.

Second religion   And they should see to it and
she should see to it.

| Third religion | She should see to it. |
| Fourth religion | She sees to it. |

Fourth religion   A fifth only of the bananas
were shown.

Fourth religion   If he surprised if he was surprised if a fifth only of the bananas were shown, if all the
bananas were grown if she was surprised if they were surprised and in their surprise are they wise.

Third religion   If they are wise, if all the bananas are grown if a fifth of the bananas are shown are they
surprised, were they surprised.

Second religion   If only a fifth of the bananas
were shown, if it were known that all the bananas were
grown, if they were surprised if she was surprised, is she
wise if all the bananas are grown.

First religion   If all the bananas are grown.
If a fifth of the bananas are shown. If they are wise. If she
feels surprise if a fifth of all the bananas are shown.

First religion   They look and see and so they
know that they do not share in their attention. And why
does she show that she does share in their attention.

Second religion   And why do they share in their

attention and why do they show that they know that they share in their attention. They share in their attention.

Third religion   And why does she share in their attention. Why does she show that she knows that she shares in attention. Shares in their attention. Share in attention. Why does she show that she does that she knows that she shares the attention so that she does know that she does share in their attention.

Fourth religion   She could know that she could share in their attention.

Fourth religion   If they stop it if they say they have received it indeed they have received it and they have stopped they have stopped it indeed they have received it they find that they need to receive it. Indeed they do. Compare what there is to say with where they stay. Compare. I find that they are kneeling there where the water is flowing.

Third religion   If she is to receive and to stop if indeed she is to stop it if indeed she is to receive if indeed can she need it can she receive it, need she stop it, can she furnish a house as well.

Second religion   Can she find that she is kind can she receive it can she need it can she stop, can they need it can they stop it can they receive and and can they need it.

First religion   Does she see the grass grown four times yearly can she receive it can she stop can she need it can she receive can she need it can she receive it.

First religion   I can appoint I can point out this way.

Second religion   She can point out that way she can appoint the delay.

Third religion   Can they appoint, can I say can they point in this way.

Fourth religion She can be disappointed at their
delay and she can point this way in this way.
Fourth religion Can you prepare the house so
that she can furnish the house as well.
Third religion Can you prepare the earth so
that the grass can grow nearly four times yearly.
Second religion Is the water flowing so that they
kneel there where the water is flowing.
First religion Can she prepare the way so that
one fifth of the bananas are shown when all the bananas are
grown.
First religion She can be cherished.
First religion She can prepare in that way.
First religion How can the first be the first.
And the second be the second. And the third be the third.
And the fourth be the fourth. How can the fourth be the
fourth.
Fourth religion She made them stay.
Third religion She came in this way.
Second religion They came and they were there
where there was place for them.
First religion She came in the same way.
First religion At first they came to stay. At
first they care when they go away. At first they stare and
in this way they stay. At first they go away.
At first she can go away. At first she can go away or she can
be sent away. At first she can be sent in this way. At first
she can stay. At first what may she do at first. At first what
can she do.
What they can do she can do.
She can do what they do. What do they do.
How do you do.
Second religion What can they say. What can

be said the second day. And how can you say a second and not stay. How can you how can they second them in that way. Secondly they stay. Secondly they do know when they stay.

Secondly they go away. If they go away and stay do they stay away. Every second of the day.

Third religion   The third makes one third, one third and she may stay. One third and if she may begin in that way she can go or she may even be sent away.

One third stay. Indeed one third do stay. Or do they stay. Or do they stay away. Or do they stay. Or does she stay. Or is she sent away. Or is she away. Or is she to stay.

Fourth religion   Four and no more. Did you say four. Did she say four. Are there more. If she stays and a fourth more. Two fourths more. She will stay, she will not leave she will say she will stay.

Fourth religion   More and more every day.

Third religion   In this way.

Second religion   Because they may.

First religion   She easily may.

First religion   She may not easily stay. If she does go away will she take with her where will she take her with her.

Second religion   If they stay if they go away will they go away there where we remember to have seen that there were no difficulties.

Third religion   If she does not or if she does not go away, or if she goes away or if she comes to stay, I do not think so. I do not think so. Or I do not think so.

Fourth religion   If she does go away, yes, if she does go away, yes if she does go away, if she does stay if she stays yes if she does stay.

Fourth religion   To send, to pretend to offend, to

descend and to descend, to contend, to defend, to mend, to descend to defend to contend to tend, to attend, yes I will say so.

Third religion   To receive and to believe, to believe and to deceive to establish and to blemish to arrange and not to change and please how can she come to please and how can she not come and how can she not please, how can she especially please very especially please.

Second religion   Can they rejoice, who can rejoice, have they the choice, who can choose, can they exchange, who can exchange, can they prepare with whom can they share what they prepare.

First religion   She has brought it here, she has brought it to bear on that, she has brought it there and she has brought to bear there on that. She has brought it to bear on this. She has brought it here she has brought it here to bear on this.

First religion   Now I call out, call out and she calls out and I hear and she calls out and she hears what is said. Now I call out and I hear what is said. Now she calls out and I hear what is said.

Second religion   If in walking they hear what is said if they hear what is said and if they are walking when they hear what is said they said no they said we are not prepared they are not to prepare for it. They are not ready to prepare. They prepare it. They say prepare it.

Third religion   If either of them or if either one of them, if she sees to it that she walks and prepares, that she prepares and that she cares, that she cares and prepares if she sees to it that she cares, if she sees to it that she prepares that it is prepared if she sees to it that it is prepared.

Fourth religion   Does she hear it does she hear them does she walk and does she hear them does she hear

194

them as she walks and does she care to prepare does she prepare to care does she care and does she prepare.

Fourth religion   A fourth religion and what not and a figure with a sheep with a cock and with a flower.

Third religion   And if not why not and a figure with a cock a figure with a sheep, a figure with a flower.

Second religion   And indeed why not if there are figures and if the figures have sheep and if the figures have cocks and if the figures have flowers.

First religion   If the figure is the one that has the sheep, if the figure is the one that has the cock if the figure is the one that has the flower if the figure and there is no other need for it.

First religion   If you can see accidents birds and messages, if you can see that you are not young and had better remain so, as you are, remain so as you are, if you can see accidents birds and messages if you can remain so as you are, count less count eight or nine. To count less brings her back to their finding that she was kneeling there where the water was flowing and the glass if it is prepared abundantly covers it all. It is made to roll and cover easily spring vegetables.

Second religion   If you can see leaves wood and disturbances if they can see disturbances leaves and wood if they can see green grass growing nearly four times yearly if they have felt that it will all be covered by wool made in the North from sheep who feed in the south if they know that it will all be covered here where the grass can grow nearly four times yearly then they have their land.

Third religion   If she can see melons and smoke and violence, if she can feel that no one kneels there where the stable is built by an Italian who has not built it but is

195

the stableman in it. If she can feel that she can see smoke and disturbances and she can see melons and smoke and disturbances can she see me. If you see me God bless the moon and God bless me.

Fourth religion   Will she see to it that she can see a reader a pleasure and an alarm. Will she see to it that there is no harm in that that she can furnish a house as well. Very well. She can furnish a house as well.

Fourth religion   Sixteen fifty four and seven, all good children can even see to it that they meant to be told what was not wonderfully told. Are they bold then.

Third religion   Fifty four
                        Sixty seven
                        One hundred and nine and nearly every time they fasten it back.

Second religion   Eighty four and eighty four did they ever before have such an opportunity of colouring bananas. No one colours bananas I say no one colours bananas.

First religion   Nine and seven do not make fifty four any more, nor did they ever.

First religion   To continue.

Second religion   We continue.

Third religion   They can continue.

Fourth religion   We can continue.

Fourth religion   We do continue.

Third religion   We continue too.

Second religion   We continue to continue.

First religion   We do continue.

First religion   Climb a wall all climb a wall. All climb a wall. All can climb a wall. They all can climb a wall. What is a wall. A wall is not a well. Very well and was she satisfied with water.

Second religion   Very prettily. She very prettily makes three of them, one of them and another of them and two of them. Three of them actually see the tree. I see the tree and the tree sees me. Very prettily too. Very prettily.

Third religion   And was there a place called a plan, and was the plan a place were there were four roads and were four roads only two roads and are two roads four roads. And a plan. We do not plan grain. By grain we mean seeds and by seeds we mean flowers. Plan and four roads and two roads are four roads.

Fourth religion   I do believe in warming water. I do believe in warming water I do believe in warming water I do believe in warming water.

Fourth religion   An extra account.

Third religion   On account.

Second religion   On their account.

First religion   To count.

First religion   In a way a false winter they say. In a way.

Second religion   A false winter if a winter is false does it mean that it is warm and seems cold, that it is cold and seems warm, is there any harm in a false winter is there any charm in a false winter.

Third religion   If a false winter seems warm if a false winter is warm, if a winter is false is there any reason for alarm, is there any reason for alarm if a winter seems warm, if a winter is warm if there is a false winter in winter.

Fourth religion   If there is an opening which leads to a street does that mean that there can be or can there seem to be as there does seem to be a false winter and not so greatly not very gently and yet a false winter if

197

it is warm would it not be so gently, it would not be so it would not be gently so it would not be so gently.

Fourth religion   And now she will see that she says that she can see and looking she can see that she saw it rightly. It was a green frog and very much such as it would be if it had been painted.

Third religion   It was a necessity it was necessarily a decision it was necessary to decide if it was a blade and if it was a frog and beside it was necessary to decide.

Second religion   It was more than necessary to decide if there was beside anything beside that which she saw there. She saw there what was there.

First religion   If she looked and if she sighed she did not sigh she did decide, she decided that she saw what was there and beside that there was nothing to see there.

First religion   Feathers and first religion. She feels the first religion freely, she feels it freely and she does not need security for it. She does not need security and security is scarcely seen while no one scatters out of her way in this way.

Second religion   She surrenders herself there and selections are easily made, indeed selections are easily made. Select me. I select you. Select her. I select her. Select them I select them. In this way not by her delay, she does not delay them.

Third religion   To be thirty, thoroughly to be thirty and then to be satisfied beside who is satisfied when she is satisfied and if she is satisfied who is satisfied beside. Who is it that is satisfied beside.

Fourth religion   From religion for there are four religions, and for religion what is there for religion, what is there and what is it that there is for religion. What is for religion. Four religions and she and she is needed for religion. For four religions.

For the fourth religion.

Fourth religion	Furnish the religion.
Third religion	There is a third religion.
Second religion	Sending a religion sending the

second religion. And two. Sending the second religion and two. In every language there is second and two.

First religion   One and one and one and the won, this I have begun. First and one one and then one we do not feel that in every language there is a first and one and really there is not a first and one not in every language. Not in every language is there a one, is there a first is there a first and one. First one and then another one. First one. The very first is one. One and one.

First religion   Did she earnestly pursue did she earnestly pursue this for that.

Second religion   Did she determine to do this and that.

Third religion   Did she repeatedly renew this in that.

Fourth religion   Did they undertake anew to give this for that.

Fourth religion	Did they.
Third religion	She did.
Second religion	She did realise this.
First religion	She did realise it.
First religion	What did happen.
Second religion	And what has happened.
Third religion	What is happening.
Fourth religion	What is happening to her.
Fourth religion	Are they our roses.
Third religion	Is it our dew.

Second religion   Is it our water.
First religion   Is it our garden.
Fourth religion   Is it in our garden.
Third religion   Are they on our roses.
Second religion   Is it for our water.
First religion   Is it frost or dew.
First religion   And they remain few.
Second religion   Are they there anew.
Third religion   Are these for you.
Fourth religion   And can you.
Fourth religion   Many words mention this.
Third religion   And are there any words in
which to say this.
Second religion   Why do they say that there.
First religion   Why do they say this when
they are here.
First religion   Alphabets are a way of say
a b c.
Second religion   Alphabets are a way of ex-
pressing love for you and for me.
Third religion   Alphabets are in the way.
Fourth religion   Alphabets are as one may say
alphabets to-day.
Fourth religion   Mutterings begin when roses are
given away.
Third religion.   Roses are not given away in this
way.
Second religion   No roses are given away.
First religion   Roses are necessary and they are
given away in this way.
First religion   And now for an address.
Second religion   And for redress.
Third religion   And for excess.

200

Fourth religion	And for authority.
Fourth religion	I have neglected I have not neg-

lected she has not neglected nor has she been neglected nor indeed does she neglect it.

Third religion	Extra pieces here and there, ex-

tra pieces are here and extra pieces are there and she can care for the extra pieces.

Second religion	Can there be really flowers here

when sisters strangers and they themselves need it.

First religion	And naturally when, when do

they naturally arrange for this and for that and when do they nearly arrange for it and for them to be near.

First religion	First a religion.
Second religion	Second a religion.
Third religion	Third a religion.
Fourth religion	Fourth a religion.
Fourth religion	Fourth in religion.
	Third in religion.
	Third in religion.
Second religion	Second in religion.
First religion	First in religion.
First religion	First in religion what do you

say when a sheep thrusts a lamb out of her way and a lamb is in the way when the lamb is thrust out of the way.

Second religion	Second in religion when you say

that it is needful to ripen pumpkins in this way.

Third religion	Third in religion when they say

that in this way they are gay.

Fourth religion	Fourth religion when they

spread out there where oranges are not rare.

Fourth religion	Do not despair.
Third religion	Do please care.
Second religion	Do do share.

First religion   Do they dedicate themselves to
this preparation.
First religion   I know how to play hide and
seek. And so does he, and so does she and so do they and so
do the others.
First religion   Mention this to them at the
same time.
First religion   No no she says no and I clap
my hands and say no no too.
First religion   Do you appear to be interested
in the south and its cultivation. Are you as you appear to
be interested in the development of the cultivation of the
south and of vegetables and animals and trees and shrubs
and climates. Are you as you appear to be humanly free.
Are you as you appear to be deeply interested in the cultivation of the earth and in the growth of vegetables trees
flowers shrubs and climate. Are you as you seem to be. Are
you humanly free as you seem to me to be. Are you free to
be interested in the cultivation of vegetables flowers trees
and shrubs.
Second religion   Is she rarely seen to be between
the houses. Is she very rarely seen to be between the houses
and in this way is she very rarely seen to mean to all of
them, to mean to be to all of them what all of them seem to
all of them to mean to any of them. Does she rarely mean
to be seen between the houses by all of them. Does she rarely
mean to seem to be seen by all of them between the houses
of all of them. Does she rarely mean does she mean very
rarely to be between the houses and does she mean not to
be seen to be between the houses. She does not mean to be
between the houses.
Third religion   In this way we cannot find this
to say.

Fourth religion   In their houses if their houses meet, houses do meet the street, if their houses meet, if between their houses it as it were houses meet, and houses are on the street, how can she seem to be between the houses. How can she seem not to mean to be between the houses. As between houses. How can she mean not to be between houses. I wonder how she can mean not to seem to be between houses. I can wonder how she can mean this about not being in between houses.

Fourth religion	Rapidly prepare for days.
Third religion	Rapidly prepare this for days.
Second religion	To rapidly prepare days.
First religion	To rapidly prepare for days.
Fourth religion	To repair here and to repair there.
Third religion	To repair.
Second religion	When can you repair this.
First religion	Where can you repair.
First religion	We have two wishes.
Second religion	We have to wish.
Third religion	We have two wishes and we have to wish.
Fourth religion	We have to wish and we have two wishes.
Fourth religion	May she be eager.
Third religion	If she were more eager may she be more eager might she be more eager.
Second religion	If she were more than eager she might be more eager.
First religion	If she were eager and she was eager, she was eager and she might be eager. She might be more eager. She might be more than eager. She might be more eager.

First religion   He does not hesitate to leave
and to come she does not hesitate to leave and to come. She
does not hesitate to leave and to come.
Second religion   She does not hesitate to leave.
She does not hesitate and if she did hesitate she would not
hesitate to leave nor would she hesitate to come. She would
not hesitate either to leave nor to come.
Third religion   Come then.
Fourth religion   To come then.
Fourth religion   She did not hesitate to come.
Third religion   She did not hesitate nor did she
hesitate to come.
Second religion   She did not leave she did not
come she did not leave to come.
First religion   Neither did she leave nor did
she come.
First religion   We said. He said it certainly.
Second religion   If she was discovered being
very able to say that.
Third religion   If she meant to be absolutely
reverberating.
Fourth religion   If they were excelled alto-
gether.
Fourth religion   I know that you do know.
Third religion   This and that and more.
Second religion   She had it as if she had made it.
Third religion   Who has said it who has had
it who has had it who has heard it, who has heard it, who
has hid it, who has hid it, who has held it, who has held
it, who has it.
First religion   Steadily to colour stockings,
very steadily indeed and steaming it there any steam I wonder and do you plan to add this here.

Second religion   Do you plan to add to this and
do you fairly furnish a reason for it or do you doubt the
use of horses here.
Third religion   Do you doubt that houses are
to be used at all and are you not silenced by lack of sound.
He sounds as if he heard it.
Fourth religion   He sounds as if he heard it as
readily as if he had been able to furnish it to himself as
well.
Fourth religion   And then and then very well
then.
Third religion   When do you intend to send
it again.
Second religion   It is far easier to realise that she
is able to sing.
First religion   Not really for very far for them
to hear a motor horn.
First religion   For them to hear theirs.
Second religion   For them not to hear it.
Third religion   For them when they do hurry it.
Fourth religion   For them then.
Fourth religion   And for them then.
Third religion   I have heard water and negroes
and children and electricity.
Second religion   And they need furs and wax and
light and rapidity.
First religion   And do they inhabit the houses.
First religion   Excellently this time.
Second religion   And very well for rice.
Third religion   And do they please her enough.
Fourth religion   Excellent fires which burn bam-
boos in trees.
Fourth religion   And now for this there.

Third religion	Is it nearly so situated is it nearly
so nearly situated.	
Second religion	He had found it to be there.
First religion	Where.
First religion	As to burning bamboos.
Second religion	She might easily think that
there was no reason for their being richer there.	
Third religion	Where.
Fourth religion	Where they grow vegetables so
plentifully.	
Fourth religion	If you courtesy.
Second religion	If you hold a hat on your head.
Third religion	If they are not told.
Fourth religion	Across to me.
Fourth religion	She walked across to me.
Third religion	And what did she see.
Second religion	What did she say to me.
First religion	When she walked across to me.
First religion	I need not tell you that I see the
moon and the moon sees me God bless the moon and God	
bless me which is you.	
Second religion	She need not tell me star light
star bright I wish I may I wish I might have the wish I wish	
to-night. And I have not told you what it was.	
Third religion	I wish I was a fish with a great
big tail. A polly wolly doodle a lobster or a whale. And I	
am certain no one is deceived.	
Fourth religion	Very well.
Fourth religion	If you know that a town is small
that the houses are enormous and tall that every one is very	
rich and you do not see any one fall nor indeed do you	
see any one at all tell me what is the name of the town.	
First religion	Cavaillon.

Second religion	If you find narrow streets and wonderful trees and plenty of seclusion and very little ease.
First religion	What is the name of this town.
First religion	Cavaillon.
Second religion	If you can describe sacks. How do you describe Romans.
Third religion	And Paulines.
Fourth religion	We rode into this.
Fourth religion	To-day.
Third religion	When.
Second religion	Morning or afternoon.
First religion	Before or afterwards.
First religion	To very nearly please.
Second religion	To very nearly please me.
Third religion	To very nearly please me here.
Fourth religion	To please me.

FINIS